Time came in, with its black and shrieking wind.

There were others in the black wind with her. Half people. Bodies and souls flying through Time. But not me! cried Annie, without sound. I learned my lesson—you taught me! Just because you *can* go through Time doesn't mean you *should*.

W9-CCC-090

ALSO AVAILABLE IN LAUREL-LEAF BOOKS:

BOTH SIDES OF TIME, *Caroline B. Cooney*
THE FACE ON THE MILK CARTON, *Caroline B. Cooney*
WHATEVER HAPPENED TO JANIE?, *Caroline B. Cooney*
DRIVER'S ED, *Caroline B. Cooney*
TWENTY PAGEANTS LATER, *Caroline B. Cooney*
OPERATION: HOMEFRONT, *Caroline B. Cooney*
THE CAR, *Gary Paulsen*
THE TENT, *Gary Paulsen*
THE RIFLE, *Gary Paulsen*
THE GIVER, *Lois Lowry*

OUT OF
TIME

Caroline B. Cooney

Published by
Bantam Doubleday Dell Books for Young Readers
a division of
Bantam Doubleday Dell Publishing Group, Inc.
1540 Broadway
New York, New York 10036

If you purchased this book without a cover you should be aware that this book is stolen property. It was reported as "unsold and destroyed" to the publisher and neither the author nor the publisher has received any payment for this "stripped book."

Copyright © 1996 by Caroline B. Cooney

All rights reserved. No part of this book may be reproduced or transmitted in any form or by any means, electronic or mechanical, including photocopying, recording, or by any information storage and retrieval system, without the written permission of the Publisher, except where permitted by law. For information address Delacorte Press, New York, New York 10036.

The trademark Laurel-Leaf Library® is registered in the U.S. Patent and Trademark Office.
The trademark Dell® is registered in the U.S. Patent and Trademark Office.

ISBN: 0-440-21933-7

RL: 5.7

Reprinted by arrangement with Delacorte Press

Printed in the United States of America

August 1997

10 9 8 7 6 5 4

OUT OF TIME

∾ CHAPTER 1 ∾

Annie Lockwood had not forgotten about Strat, of course. But she had forgotten about him this morning. She woke up fast, and was out of bed in seconds, standing in front of her closet and changing every fashion decision she had made yesterday.

Her American history class was off to New York City today. Forty minutes by train. Since they were going to the United Nations first, the teacher wanted them to look decent, by which he meant that the girls were not to follow the current fad of wearing men's boxer shorts on the outside of their ripped jeans and the boys were not to follow the current fad of wearing T-shirts so obscene that strangers would ask what town the class was from, so as to be sure they never accidentally went and lived there.

Actually, it was nice to have an excuse to look good.

1

Grunge had hit the school system hard, and those who preferred pretty, or even clean, were out of the loop.

Annie had a long, dark blue dress, a clinging knit bought for a special occasion. It didn't stand out from the crowd, but Annie did when she wore it. She put on the hat she'd found at the secondhand store. It was a flattened bulb of blue velvet. How jauntily it perched over her straight dark hair. Perfect. (Unless she lost her courage and decided the hat, any hat, especially this hat, was pathetic.)

She whipped downstairs to get her brother's opinion. Tod generally did not bother with words. If he despised her clothes, he would gag or pretend to pass out, or maybe even threaten her with butter throwing. (Butter left out on the counter made a wonderful weapon, especially if it got in your sister's hair.) If Tod liked her outfit, though, he would shrug with his eyebrows. This was a great accolade, and meant she looked okay, even if she was his sister.

She was kind of fond of Tod, which was a good thing, since they were the only people left in their family.

Annie and Tod hadn't bothered with breakfast since Mom had left. Breakfast was only worth having if somebody else made it for you.

The house was literally colder without Mom, because Mom had always gotten up way earlier and turned up the thermostat, so when Annie and Tod came down to the kitchen, it was toasty and welcoming. Even though Mom's commute to New York meant she'd caught her train before Annie and Tod came down, they always used to feel Mom in the house. They could smell coffee she had perked and hot perfumed moisture from her shower. Orange juice was always poured, cereal and milk out, toast sitting in the slots waiting to be lowered. On the fridge was always a Post-it to each child:

ANNIE—ace that history test, love you, Mom.

TOD—don't forget your permission slip, love you, Mom.

But "always" was over.

In the kitchen (where the front of the refrigerator was bare) her brother was drinking orange juice straight from the carton. Since she was doing the same thing these days, Annie could hardly yell at him. She just waited her turn. He smiled, orange juice pouring into his mouth, which caused some to dribble onto the linoleum.

"Nice manners," said Annie, and the word *manners* triggered a rush of memories. There were too many, she didn't want this—

Her head split open. Time came in, with its black and shrieking wind.

There were others in the black wind with her. Half people. Bodies and souls flying through Time. But not me! cried Annie, without sound. I learned my lesson—you taught me! Just because you *can* go through Time doesn't mean you *should*.

Time let go.

She was just a panting girl in a cold room.

3

"Wow," said her brother, folding the carton tips together before handing over the orange juice, as if this were a germ protection device. "That was so weird, Annie."

"What was?" She did not know how she could talk. Oxygen had been ripped from her lungs.

"Your hair," he said nervously. "It curled by itself."

For a moment their eyes met, his full of questions and hers full of secrets. "Do you like my hat?" she said, because hair curled by Time was a tough subject.

"Yeah. Makes you look like a deranged fashion model."

Deranged. What if Tod was right? What if she was on some grim and teetery edge, and she was going to fall off her own sanity? What if she landed, not in another century like the last time, but in some other, hideously confused, mind?

Annie ran back upstairs, to get away from the collapse of Time and the sharp eyes of her brother. To get closer to Strat.

The image of Strat had faded over the months. When she thought of him now, it was loosely, like silver bracelets sliding on her arms.

Sometimes she went to Stratton Point, alone with the wind, but even Strat's mansion was only memory. Torn down. Nothing now but a scar on a hill. Annie would make sure there was no living person around—no footprints in the snow—no ski tracks—no cars parked below with the windows rolled down—and she'd shout out loud, "Strat! Strat! I love you!"

But of course nobody answered, and Time did not

open. There was just a teenage girl shrieking for a nonexistent teenage boy.

This morning, in her bedroom, there was nothing wrong, nothing out of place. No clues to Time or any other secret. Piles of clothing, paperbacks, and CDs were right where she had left them, her drawers half open and her closet doors half shut. But today must be the day! thought Annie. That falling was Time's warning.

"Hi, Strat," she whispered to the mirror, as if he and his century were right behind the glass, and the opening of Time was ready.

The Strattons, she thought suddenly, had a Manhattan town house. I've been going to their beach mansion —their Connecticut summer place. But what if the passage back through Time is in New York City?

Old New York rose as vividly in her mind as if she really had visited there: romantic and dark, full of velvet gowns and stamping horses and fine carriages.

She stared at herself in her full-length mirror. If Time takes me, I'll be ready. I'll be elegant and ladylike.

Of course, not in front of her history class. They must not ask questions. She stuffed the hat into her old L.L. Bean bookbag.

It was midwinter. February, to be exact, and the snowiest winter on record. Annie could wear her best boots (best in fashion, not in staying dry), which were high black leather with chevrons of velvet. She dashed into Mom's room to filch Mom's black kid gloves and her winter coat pin: a snowflake of silver, intricate as lace. Mom had ordered it from a museum catalog, which triggered such a flow of catalogs they threatened to snap the mailbox. (Tod loved this; he was always hoping for another, more explicit, *Victoria's Secret*.)

Annie had other secrets in mind. The secrets that the Strattons had carried through Time.

How many hours had Annie spent in the library since she and Strat parted forever? Combing yellow newspapers stacked in crumbling towers in the basement? Studying church records and town ledgers, hungry for a syllable about the Strattons?

Old newspapers covered Society, and the Strattons had been Society a hundred years ago. "Mr. Hiram Stratton, Jr., will soon begin his first year at Yale." "Miss Devonny Stratton will be voyaging to Paris." "Miss Harriett Ranleigh is again visiting her dear friends, the Strattons." "Mr. Walker Walkley has accepted the invitation of the Strattons to sail for several days on the family yacht."

This was proof that the Strattons were real: that Annie Lockwood really and truly had lived and loved among them.

And then, they ceased to be real. The Strattons vanished from the printed record. There was nothing written about them again. *Not ever.*

No marriage. No birth. No death. No property sold. No visitors mentioned.

The Strattons stepped off Time, leaving no tombstones, no letters and no clues.

Had Annie done that? Had she destroyed the Strattons by coming through Time and changing their lives?

What had happened to them? Where had they gone? Who had married whom?

She would never know—unless she fell through Time again and caught up.

Downstairs in the front hall, she took her mother's long formal black wool coat from its hanger. She pinned the silver snowflake on the narrow lapel. Carefully, using the violet-trimmed paper Mom kept by the hall phone, Annie wrote a note to the history teacher.

Everything in the note was a lie.

❧

Tod was putting on his ice hockey jacket, which he never zipped no matter how cold it was. Tod tapped his sister's silver snowflake. "You think it's Halloween, maybe? You're going as a grown-up?"

"Do I look weird?" she asked anxiously. No matter what century you were in, nothing was worse than being a fashion jerk.

"You look great," said her brother gravely. Tod—who never gave compliments; it was one of the principles he lived by. "But it's a pretty dressy outfit," said Tod, very casually, "for a school field trip."

This was the tricky part for Annie. Tod would still be here and would still have to face reality. Annie was sick of reality. Especially Lockwood family reality. "Tod," she said, even more casually, "if I don't come home tonight . . . don't tell Dad."

Annie was suddenly deeply terrified. What if I get trapped in Time? she thought. What if Time takes me

7

someplace else, instead of to Strat? What if he and Harriett are already married? What if they aren't?

Tod zipped his hockey jacket, which astonished her. The sound of the zipper closing was ominous, as if she were being closed out of her brother's life. "I just wonder, Annie, if you know what you're doing."

I have no idea what I am doing. Time will do it to me.

"I don't want to be a one-person family," said her brother.

"We're still a family," she said quickly. "Just scattered."

Last year, Dad had decided he had better things to do than maintain a family. He had become involved with Miss Bartten. When Mom fell apart over this, Dad said grumpily, "I'm not going to marry her. I'm not even asking for a divorce. I just want a different lifestyle."

Mom had not taken this well, especially when Dad thought he could have a different lifestyle but still bring Mom his laundry. Talk about la-la land. Dad was actually surprised when Mom destroyed his wardrobe. "By the way," Mom had said, talking over a sea of buttons no longer attached to shirts, "my brokerage firm is opening an office in Tokyo."

"Neat," Dad had said, clearly wondering if his credit cards were maxed out or if he could afford all new clothes. Sleeves were now being ripped off to join the buttons.

"They've asked me to go Japan for a month to set things up."

"Congratulations," Dad had said. There was no point

in hoping Miss Bartten would mend those torn clothes. The Miss Barttens of this world are not domestic.

Mom raised her voice, trying to tap into Dad's consciousness. "So you need to move back into this house full time for the month of February and take care of Annie and Tod while I'm in Tokyo."

"Sure," Dad said, and escaped from the house with his body intact, if not his clothing.

Annie and Tod knew their father had not been listening. He hadn't heard the word *Tokyo* or the word *Japan* and he definitely had not heard the sentence requiring him to live at home again for a month. Brother and sister had looked at each other with perfect understanding: they were about to be on their own for four weeks.

So Annie didn't want to think about Tod left all alone here. Not that he wasn't mature enough. He had his driver's license, and all, but still—he would be alone. And neither parent realized it.

I should confess, thought Annie, so that if something does happen, Tod will know. He deserves answers. *If something does happen* . . . like what? What do I think will go wrong? If Time takes me again, I'll be going to Strat. Won't I? He loved me so! Doesn't love conquer all? Or have I been lying about what really happened in 1895? I lie to everybody else. Am I lying to myself now too?

She turned to tell her brother some of the truth, but he was not there. Tod had gone on to school. She was alone in the house. There was nothing there but the hum of the refrigerator and the click of a clock.

Annie shivered.

Could people come and go from real life without her noticing them? Was she too busy noticing unreal people?

She almost tore up the note she had written to her teacher. It was too foolish.

But instead she tucked the note in her palm, and slid her hand into her glove, and there the note lay waiting, papery and warm and full of the future. *Or the past.*

Shackles work.

Strat stared at the chains on his wrists. He was young and strong—and chained.

He was willing to admit to anything they wanted now. He would make any promise if they'd just let him loose. "What year is it?" he asked the doctor.

Patient does not know year, the doctor wrote in Strat's casebook.

"I'm fine," Strat said to the doctor. "This is a mistake."

"Really? Your father chose this, you recall."

"I disobeyed my father. I was wrong. I won't do it again. I'm not insane. I agree that my father knows everything."

"Do you?"

"Please let me out."

The doctor shook his head. "You are a danger to yourself and others, Mr. Stratton."

Strat said, "Would you permit me more than one

hour a day of exercise? Please? I promise to be good. I promise not to try to scale the walls."

"You are fortunate," said the doctor, "that your father is wealthy. He has paid for a private asylum, where you will get all the help you need. Right now you need restraint, not exercise."

Strat's body screamed for exercise. Every joint shrieked to be moved, every muscle cried out to be swung and changed. But arguing would go in the casebook, and the casebook decided everything. "Did I get any letters?" he said, struggling for courtesy, for a normal smile. He must look normal at all costs. "Did Harriett answer me yet?"

The doctor smiled.

The doctor and Ralph, the attendant, moved Strat back to the crib. He fought, but they who owned the key to the shackles were in charge, no matter how young and strong Strat was.

The crib was an adult-size bed with barred sides and a cleverly fastened canvas lid. Strat could not get out. He could not undo the canvas. He could not sit up. It was a torture chamber with a mattress. They removed the chains once he was inside. False freedom. He could do nothing with those hands, so he used the only other tool available to him.

Bites canvas, wrote the doctor, and then the doctor left.

"No!" screamed Strat. "No, don't go, please, please, please, you're a civilized man, please . . ."

The door closed behind the doctor.

The building had been constructed as a lunatic asylum. Its walls were very thick and its doors very solid.

Ralph the attendant smiled. The wider Ralph smiled, the more danger the patient was in.

"Please, Ralph," said Strat, "please let me write another letter. This will be to my sister, Devonny. I'll give you all the money I have."

Ralph laughed. "I already have all the money you have."

Strat had no pride left. "Devonny will give you money. Just please let me have a pencil and paper."

Ralph walked slowly to the doctor's desk. The other four patients in the room watched to see if Ralph would actually bring a piece of paper, a pencil, a stamp, and an envelope. If there was hope for Strat, perhaps there was hope for them too.

Strat's heart was pounding. If he could get Devonny to come . . . or Harriett . . . or his mother . . .

But Ralph came back with Strat's casebook. Ralph couldn't read, of course; a lunatic asylum did not hire the sort of person who had conquered reading, but Ralph could recognize. Ralph held up the brown leather journal in which the doctor's spidery handwriting made daily entries. Ralph turned the pages midair, so not just Strat, but also the other patients, could see each page.

Every letter Strat had written begging for help was pasted into the notebook.

Not one had ever been mailed.

Sean picked Annie up in his latest vehicle. Sean was working at an auto repair shop now. He was in his glory. He no longer had to struggle to purchase cars; he could just slap on a dealer plate and drive off the lot with his prize.

They hadn't dated since Annie met Strat. (Not that Sean had the slightest idea who Strat was.) But Sean went right on adoring Annie, accepting the fact that he had no purpose in her life other than to give her rides in bad weather.

Sometimes Annie was ashamed of this, but not today. She wanted her boots dry and the hem of her long dress out of the snow. "Hi, Sean."

"Hi, Annie. Wow. Some outfit."

"This is how people dress to go into New York," said Annie defensively. She was worried about how the other girls would dress. She didn't want to stand out or get teased. But these clothes would move across Time with her.

"Hear from your mom?" said Sean. "She like Tokyo?"

"Yes," said Annie, though her last conversation with Mom had been at the airport, saying good-bye.

("Get us good presents, Mom," Tod had teased, hugging his mother gently. Mom was very teary, unable to leave her children. "We'll slaughter Miss Bartten for you," Tod offered. "Think of the alibi you'll have. Continents and oceans." Mom had managed to smile. "Make it painful," she told Tod. They shook on it.)

What if I'm gone for a long time? thought Annie. What if Tod has to tell Mom, and she's in Japan, and finds out I'm missing, and—

"We're here," said Sean. He smiled at Annie. Sean was a very good-looking young man. It was too bad he had no personality to go with it. Annie patted Sean's knee and Sean sighed. "How come I get pats, and never kisses?"

"I guess I'm not feeling very romantic these days," said Annie, which was one of her larger lies. She had thought of nothing but romance since meeting Strat. She worried about the extent and number of her lies. Was this a sign of insanity? Would she wake up one day, gently tranquilized, her scattered family gathered around her bed in a psychiatric unit?

"See you tonight," said Sean, and Annie was horrified. Had she promised Sean a date or something? But she needed tonight! If Time came . . .

"Don't look as if I threw up on you," said Sean irritably. "I'm just picking you up at the 6:03 train."

"I might not be on it," said Annie quickly. "I might stay at Mom's New York apartment."

Sean's jaw dropped. "I didn't know your mother kept an apartment in New York."

"Ever since Dad moved out," Annie lied. She would get caught on this one. Or maybe not. It was amazing, the number of lies you could tell without being noticed. The whole thing was in carrying it off.

She got on the train, lifting her skirts above the slush. The rest of the class had boarded and she was last. There was an uneven number of kids, and Annie

14

sat alone. She would have minded terribly last year; she would have been crushed and humiliated and ready to die. Now she was delighted. She could think of Time and the Strattons.

The train lurched noisily toward Grand Central Station.

They stopped at Greenwich and Rye and Mamaroneck. At Larchmont and New Rochelle and Mount Vernon.

Don't do this, Annie said to herself. You're just going because you're selfish and curious. Don't pretend it's love. You know perfectly well Strat had to marry Harriett. She needed him most. You knew it then, you know it now. Don't you go back there and wreck that. And think of your own family. Things aren't bad enough already?

Annie felt much better after accusing herself of terrible things.

Besides, Time gave her no choice, did it? It would grab her by the ankles and throw her through the century.

And then I'll know, thought Annie. I'll have the answers. And that's what everybody wants from Life. The Answers.

❦

From her chair on the glassed-in porch, Harriett looked at winter. Absolutely nothing happened in the Adirondack Mountains except weather. Frigid, twenty-below weather.

Indoors, the coal stove was red hot and the windows

had steamed up. The stove was a tall potbelly with peculiar side ridges. Moss, the nurse, had explained that it was a laundry stove, and the ledges would hold two dozen flatirons. The heating stove had exploded, Moss said, and this was the substitute. Harriett was not comforted by the thought of a stove exploding.

But Harriett was kept outdoors, so that clear, clean, cold air would climb into her lungs and scour out the consumption. She was wrapped in blankets and furs, a hot soapstone tucked beneath her feet. She would rather be inside with an exploding stove. They could call it a cure porch if they wanted, but Harriett, personally, called it torture.

Harriett had had a cough the previous winter and spring, but most people did, so she thought little of it. Even though she felt feverish every afternoon, she said nothing. She loved the pink in her cheeks. So romantic. And she was in love, wearing the sapphire ring Strat had given her, and was thinking of nothing but marriage.

The loss of weight, too, was delightful. Being slender and willowy was so much better than being solid. A child-woman is far more attractive than a womanly woman. It was relief to be frail, as a woman should be. All went well until one day the coughing was so severe that Harriett hemorrhaged, drenching handkerchiefs with blood.

This was consumption. Lungs that ate the body instead of air.

Naturally, one lied. Admit that a member of the family had consumption? Not likely. It would be the end of party invitations.

Still, only the very best people got consumption, and of course they had to have the very best treatment. Clear Pond featured a terribly expensive and exclusive cure.

There were "up" cottages, where patients could get out of bed, but Harriett was "on trays." Meals were carried to her because she had to be motionless. Her lungs must never struggle. Up patients could have activities: picnics in summer and sleigh rides in winter. Poor Harriett could only obey the cure and hope to stay alive.

Hope was strong in the heart of Harriett Ranleigh. She had plans! A life—a wonderful man—their perfect future together. Surely a cough would not end that forever.

She was not even permitted to use a pencil, since mental exercise was known to be as tiring as physical exercise. But Harriett composed a diary in her mind, as carefully and grammatically as if somebody really would read it.

I am afraid, she wrote in her mind. Why won't Strat answer my letters? How could he read those sentences I dictated to Moss, and not come to me? How could he be so hard of heart?

I am afraid of the weather too. How the wind screams. How the cold mountains stare. If I die, they will put me in that ground, and I will be cold forever. Is this your design, God? Have you chosen death for me?

God, don't you understand? I have a design too! I want to marry Strat and have babies and keep a home!

But only the wind replied, shrieking around the icicles.

They all had pet icicles; Harriett's was three feet long, but Beanie's was nearly four. An infinitely superior icicle, Beanie like to say smugly, as I am an infinitely superior person.

Harriett yearned for the day's visits. Charlie and Beanie could go skylarking and they would tell her about their activities. Charlie's cure was going well; he was actually permitted a ten-minute walk. Charlie was so slender as to be nonexistent, but in his bright-hued winter woolens, he looked puffy and plump.

Beanie and Charlie joined her on the glass porch, exhausted from the brief walk across the snow. Moss, the nurse, quickly tucked them into waiting furs and brought cups of hot tea to wrap cold fingers around.

Charlie rolled himself a cigarette and promptly set fire to his own sheets. Everybody was used to this and he was thrown a snowball with which to put it out.

Harriett whispered, "I still haven't heard from Strat."

They looked at her gently. Everybody knew that her fiancé had not once written or visited. Even Harriett's enormous fortune was not bringing Strat to her side. He was handsome. The finely framed photograph of him that she kept by her bed would have made any girl's heart pound. Probably had. Strat, it would seem, was busy with other hearts.

The students were packed tight in a hallway in the
United Nations building listening (or pretending to listen) to a woman discuss the Middle East situation. I'd
better not go through Time right now, thought Annie.
We don't need an Annie Lockwood situation.

But nothing happened.

They wrapped up the United Nations, they bought
roasted chestnuts or cappuccino or hotdogs at sidewalk
stands, they took a bus to South Street Seaport, they
steeped themselves in maritime history, and nothing
happened.

Annie had been so sure Time was coming for her.
The little note she had written to explain her absence
was stupid and futile.

Annie looked at the twenty kids who thought they
knew her. What would they say if they found out she
was trying to step across a century? What would they
say if they found out she really and truly believed she
could do it?

They would lock me up, she thought. I'd be in a
straitjacket.

She glared at New York, which was doing its best for
everybody except her.

I know what! I have to get in position. I have to be
on the right street, so all Time has to do is shift me
through the century, not to another place.

She knew the Manhattan address; she had found it in
a society report.

Okay, so I lied when I said I was going to let Time

19

handle it, thought Annie. So I'm going to help Time out a little. I'll dump my bookbag, too twentieth century, put on my squishy blue hat, all ladies wore hats in the nineteenth century, and find the corner of Fifty-second Street and Fifth Avenue.

She slid into a McDonald's line next to Heather. Once they had been inseparable—the kind of junior-high girlfriends who cannot get through the evening without an hour on the phone. Now Heather was just Heather, a nice girl Annie had once known. "Heather," whispered Annie, "would you give this note to the teacher after I'm out of here?"

Heather overreacted. "What are you talking about? Annie, it's one thing to wander off back home. This is New York City. It isn't safe. Get a grip."

"I'll be fine, I'm staying at Mom's apartment."

"Your mother has an apartment in New York? I didn't know that! Oooh, Annie, I want to stay too! Let's do something really cool."

Annie had not thought of this problem. "Next time," she said quickly. "This time I need you to cover for me."

Heather took the note dubiously. "Okay, but—"

"Thanks!" Annie took a quick look to be sure the rest of the class was thinking of french fries, and not her, and they were, so she slipped out of McDonald's, and also, she hoped, out of the twentieth century.

❦

Devonny Aurelia Victoria Stratton felt like kicking a dog.

Nothing was going right.

Every plan had failed, every person she loved was in trouble, and every hope cut down.

Devonny held Miss Lockwood responsible. Oh! If she could get her hands around Miss Lockwood's throat! Strangling was too good for her.

For Anna Sophia Lockwood had existed: everybody admitted it. Even Father admitted it. He had, after all, danced with Miss Lockwood. But only Strat had insisted that Miss Lockwood had traveled through Time to be with them.

I hate you, Anna Sophia Lockwood! thought Devonny. But I need you. "It's now or never," she said fiercely to Time. "You send her right now! Right this very minute! Do you hear me!"

There was a knock at the door and Devonny nearly fainted. Did she have such power? "Yes?" she whispered.

The door opened.

It was not Time. It was the most dangerous person she knew.

"Were you talking to someone?" he said, looking around the empty room.

Talking to Time and Miss Lockwood had put Strat in an insane asylum. Devonny must be far more careful. She managed a sweet smile, because sweetness and smiles were the only weapons a girl had in 1898. "I was practicing flirting with you," she said. She tucked her slender, silk-gloved hand into Walker Walkley's crooked arm, and prepared herself to lie and connive and do anything it took to save her brother.

21

❧ CHAPTER 2 ❧

Annie paced Fifth Avenue, trying this side and then the other, going up the near side of Fifty-second Street, and crossing over to the far side.

The city was relentlessly modern. Its cars and store windows, skyscrapers and fashions were maddeningly twentieth century. Ugly, pimpled steel and glass rose up to snow clouds so low that the buildings didn't scrape the sky; they vanished into it.

Chemical Bank, Citibank, and Japan Air. She was in her Time, all right, complete with parking meters to count car minutes.

The pout on her mouth and the frown on her forehead made her look like a street crazy with whom sane people did not make eye contact. Had Annie said to the people so carefully avoiding her that she was looking for the previous century, their worst suspicions would have been confirmed. But she was hunting, not talking.

Tod was right: in her fine black coat and her silly squashed hat, she looked like a runway model in the midst of losing her mind.

She stepped into a lobby with green marble floors and bored uniformed men and women guarding the elevators. She read the list of companies that could be found on floors two through forty. The name Stratton was not there.

I can't find the Strattons in the pages of their own society gossip and I can't find the Strattons in property records and church ledgers, but still I expect to find their name chiseled in modern buildings? I am crazy. This is proof.

She went back out. The weather had changed in only those few seconds. The wind howled down the corridors of Manhattan and icy sidewalks sucked the heat out of Annie's boots. The day had passed into night without stopping for dusk, and snow-swirled blackness strangled her.

Hunched, scurrying people jostled her, and bumped into her, and bruised her, and none of them noticed when she slipped in the slush and fell. Her skirts were soaked and her boots were ruined and her hat had vanished into the windy blast.

It took her three tries to get to her feet again, and nobody helped, or even saw.

I've lost my purse! she thought, horrified.

No purse. No money. No train ticket. No way home.

Perhaps the jostling people had been thieves, laughing at her, a pathetic suburban girl trying to find her way.

Slush filled her boots. Her mother's lovely coat was soaked and soiled. Annie Lockwood wanted nothing except to find her class and catch her train and go home. But without her purse? *If I could get to Grand Central*, she thought, *it would be warm in there, and I'd use my phone card and . . .*

And call whom? Mom was in Japan, Dad was at Miss Bartten's, Tod couldn't help. And even if she found her class, could she admit the string of lies? What excuse could she give? They'd laugh at her, or worse, take her seriously, and be kind to her little demented mind, and get the school psychiatrist in on it, and bring Mom home from Japan.

No. Whatever she did to get out of this, she had to do without confession.

She plodded street after street, legs stiff as icicles. There was no purpose to her journey anymore, but she could not find a place to stop. Her feet went on like some dreadful enchantment.

New York City splintered, and fell off itself, like pieces of a glacier. All the world except Annie moved fast, while Annie's slow feet seemed to freeze to the ground.

I have to get out of this wind, Annie thought. *I am literally freezing to death. The cold could stop my heart. Leave me frozen on the stones like an abandoned kitten.*

Halfway down a narrow side street was a row of large, elegant trees. Through the snow they seemed only half there, and half people seemed to move from half a house. The tree trunks were encircled by gold-tipped spears of black iron, part of an elaborate fence.

The half people moved toward her and, half frozen, Annie Lockwood half understood.

❧

In the lunatic asylum, the patients were being fed. "Besides, Mr. Stratton," said Ralph when he brought supper, "you write to girls. What can a female do, huh? Females is of lower intelligence than men." To prove his point, Ralph hurt Katie a little: Ralph enjoyed slapping.

Katie's family didn't want to have a deformed child around the house and had sent her to the asylum, explaining to the neighbors that their daughter had died. She might as well have.

Supper was a large bowl of lukewarm oatmeal with milk and brown sugar. For Strat, there was a spoon, but Ralph was not in the mood to give Douglass and Katie spoons. They had to put their faces in the bowl and slurp it out, like animals.

Douglass had very little brain, and his family didn't want him because he had never acquired speech. He could make noises, and after being cooped up with Douglass for so long, Strat understood the fear sound and the hope sound and the happy sound. Douglass, amazingly, was often happy. When Katie read aloud, or massaged his neck, or combed his hair, Douglass would beam at her and make his happy sound.

Really ugly people and really dumb people and really crazy people were kept in the same place.

25

It was important not to let Society know that one of the family was below standard. How would the attractive members of the family get married if such news got out? It might be in the blood, and who wanted blood that failed?

Strat's blood had failed.

His father had sentenced him to a private lunatic asylum. There were only sixty patients, so it wasn't as bad as Utica, the state asylum, with thousands. But it was just as impossible to get out of.

Katie was allowed to read, though of course the only books were the Bible or collections of sermons. Luckily the Bible had many wonderful stories, and luckily Katie liked to read aloud, so they knew by heart everything about Daniel and the lion's den and Joseph's coat of many colors.

"It's 1898, Strat," said Katie gently, finally answering his question to the long-departed doctor. "You knew that. You know you've been here nearly six months. You know we had Christmas and New Year's."

Except during the precious hour of exercise, weather was gone from their world. The inmates had no windows. No sky. No sun. Strat missed the outdoors as much as he missed the rest of the world: friends, talk, college, sailing, tennis, good food.

Where did time go, when you lost it?

He thought of the last time he had seen Anna Sophia Lockwood. She had wavered, becoming a reflection of herself. She literally slipped between his fingers. He was holding her gown and then he wasn't. He'd had a strand of her hair, and then he didn't. Nothing of her was present. Just Strat and the soft beach air. When he stopped shouting, he tried whispering, as if her vanishing were a secret and he could pull her out.

She had not wanted him to address her as Miss Lockwood, but Strat could not manage anything as familiar as Annie. So he had called her Anna Sophia, singing her two names opera style: Anna Sophia; Sophia Anna.

But the situation had been resolved, and his engagement to Harriett made public, and there had been dances and fetes and dinners, and Strat knew that if he could not have Anna Sophia—and he couldn't—he wanted Harriett. She was the history of his own life, his companion since they were children; possibly his best friend.

The subject closed to them had been Anna Sophia. Harriett had met her, of course, been nearly ruined by her, and knew Strat's theory of century changing. But Strat's heart—lost to Anna Sophia—they did not discuss. It hurt each of them far too much.

Time. Where was Harriett all this time? His sister? His mother?

"I have lost half a year," he whispered. "How many more will I lose?"

"All of them," said Katie.

❧

At the cure cottage, Beanie and Charlie were visiting Harriett.

27

Charlie, who had been an army officer, didn't want to lose any of his skills. He sat up on his cure chair with his rifle and shot apart glass bottles that his man put up on stones at the edge of the frozen pond. Come summer, nobody was going to do any barefoot wading along that part of the shore.

"In only three months," said Charlie proudly, "I have gone from being allowed ten minutes sitting up to being allowed a ten-minute sleigh ride. No doubt I shall soon be tobogganing every morning at forty below." This was a complete lie. He was getting worse. But he did not want Harriett to know.

If his dreams can come true, thought Harriett, perhaps mine will too. She allowed herself a delicious picture of life: a lovely house, a warm fire, laughing children, her beloved husband, Strat, smoking a pipe.

A fourth patient joined them. Phipps was not Harriett's favorite person, but in a society so isolated, any person was more desirable than no person.

"Hullo, Phipps," said Charlie, not very willingly.

"Hullo, Phipps," said Beanie, throwing a snowball at him. Phipps ducked and frowned at Beanie. As always, Phipps had some unpleasant subject to bring up. "I've spoken to Doctor. Supposedly our disease is caused by a little bacillus. I don't believe it. He says you can look at it through a microscope. I don't believe that either. We got sick because we offended God." This seemed to make him rather proud, as if he had accomplished something that mattered.

"How comforting," said Beanie. "In what way did I

offend God? I will have you know that I have led a blameless life."

"Nobody," said Phipps sharply, "has led a blameless life."

"Speak for yourself, you bacillus," said Beanie.

"Let's get along, please," said Moss the nurse. "Arguing isn't good for the cure. It's a strain on the lungs."

They stopped immediately. Nobody wanted a strain on the lungs. Harriett went to sleep every night now with a sandbag on her chest, to keep the ribs from moving.

When Charlie, Phipps and Beanie left, Moss gave Harriett a sponge bath, strong rubdowns with coarse towels, to improve her circulation. Then came a wonderful dinner, hot and filling. Except for the fact that she had been banished, because people were afraid of her breath, life here was good.

Moss read aloud a psalm, because Moss was a great believer.

Harriett went back and forth. There were times when she had great faith and knew God would save her, and if He didn't, heaven would nevertheless be wonderful. There were times, however, when she felt that religion was crap.

"Yea, though I walk through the valley of the shadow of death, I will fear no evil: for thou art with me," said Moss.

I, thought Harriett, do not want to walk through death until I am eighty! Do you hear me, Lord?

And then the coughing broke through.

It ripped her lungs open and blood spilled out. Moss

held her, keeping her tight, coaxing her to hang on through the agony, choke the cough down. Win. Stay alive.

When the cough ended, Moss and her helper Mario changed the sheets and blankets, again tucking Harriett in—clean, soft, white.

But would anything make her lungs clean and soft again?

This was most unusual. Dr. Wilmott himself, director of the asylum, had come to look them over.

Even more unusual, Strat was not confined, but permitted to walk about the room. It soothed him to count. He had stalked the twelve-foot-square room two hundred ninety-six times so far this afternoon. He had stepped over Melancholia and Conspiracy (two patients who really were lunatics, and whose shrieks and sobs and mutterings gave Strat headaches day and night) two hundred ninety-six times and they hadn't noticed him once. This is my life, he thought, and for the millionth time, not the two hundred ninety-sixth, he could not believe it.

"Dr. Wilmott, would you please give permission for me to exercise again today?" he said. "Sir," he added.

Dr. Wilmott shook his head. "You are a danger to yourself and others, Mr. Stratton."

If only that were true! He would love to be a danger to somebody. He would start with his father.

Strat's very own father had instructed Strat's very own Yale professor—for whom he had written the incriminating essay—to arrange the kidnapping. His professor had introduced two burly men with him as friends involved in a joke. Strat loved a good joke, as all college boys do, and willingly agreed to have his hands strapped together. Once those strapped hands were strapped to the interior of a very strangely outfitted carriage, the professor explained that Strat's beliefs in God were so incorrect that extreme measures had to be taken.

And then his father—appearing out of nowhere—glanced briefly into the conveyance. "Good," Hiram Stratton, Sr., had said. "Take him to the asylum."

Strat still thought it must be a joke, and did not fight back until it was far too late, and that, too, was counted against him—a normal person would have fought back. It was like being accused of witchery in old Massachusetts—they held you under water and if you died, then you were a normal person who needed air.

"Father," he had said, not yet scared, "what is this nonsense?"

"You need enclosure and treatment," his father had thundered. "Writing essays about *century changers* and *time crossing* and *girls who don't exist?*"

So it was about Miss Lockwood. Beautiful, funny, wonderful Anna Sophia. Even then, Strat was still in love with her—three years after she came and went, one year after his engagement to Harriett. His heart still filled with joy and loss whenever he thought of Miss Lockwood.

"You," said his very own, very angry father, "are an instrument of Satan."

"I'm your son!" Strat had shouted, but his father had not replied, and Strat was taken by force 275 miles north to the sort of place he had not dreamed existed.

Now, Dr. Wilmott said sternly to Katie, "Have you been studying your books of moral works?"

"Yes, sir."

Katie's face was so ugly, so misshapen, that the doctor did not look at her, but into the stale air above her. "You do understand," said Doctor, "that God has punished you, and there is nothing that I can do for you."

"I do understand, Dr. Wilmott, that you are a wicked, hideous, evil creation and God would never dream of working through you," said Katie calmly.

Strat froze. She must never talk to the staff like that! They would hurt her. They would punish her terribly. You had to beg from them, compliment them, you had to—

"You ugly deformed reject of society! You dare to address me like that!" hissed Dr. Wilmott. He raised his hand and Strat the athlete recognized the strength and rage in that moving arm.

But it was not Hiram Stratton, Jr., who moved to protect Katie.

It was Douglass.

Douglass stepped between the doctor and Katie and took the blow without a quiver, and took the next blow, too, and the next.

Stop it, said Strat, but to his shame no words came out.

"Stop it," said Katie to Dr. Wilmott. "You know Douglass has done no wrong."

32

Dr. Wilmott and Ralph strapped both Katie and Douglass to restraint chairs. Strat let it happen, and when they were done he said to Doctor, "I have been good, sir. May I be allowed some exercise outside?"

And Doctor smiled, and said yes.

&

"Well!" said Miss Bartten, beaming at Tod.

They were in a nice restaurant. Starched white tableclothes and linen napkins big enough to make beds with, and crystal glasses and scented candles.

"Your father and I are going to Mexico!" cried Miss Bartten. "Won't it be fun!"

Tod said to his father, "Maybe homicidal guerrillas will kidnap you. Maybe fire ants will eat off the soles off your feet. Or killer bees—"

"Stop it," said his father.

"Oh, I'm so sorry!" said Tod, hitting his forehead in remorse. "Miss Bartten, forgive me! I was being rude to you when all you did was ruin my parents' marriage. Gosh, what was I thinking of!"

"Tod," said his father through gritted teeth, "we are in public."

"Young people today have no standards," said Tod confidingly to Miss Bartten. "I mean, they actually think when a man promises to be faithful to his wife, he should do it! Can you believe that, Miss Bartten?" Tod laughed.

"*Stop it,*" said his father.

"Yes, I think we should stop," said Tod Lockwood.

"And the first thing we should stop doing is pretending that this is going to work."

Tod left the restaurant.

The point here was to upset Dad and Miss Bartten (whom he refused to call Peggy; Peggy was too friendly a name and he, Tod, was not going to be friendly; forget it) but the point also was not to let Dad notice that Annie was not here. Or if he did notice, he should be darned glad, because Annie had even more of a viper tongue than Tod.

He knew his father was saying to Miss Bartten, "Tod'll be back, he's ten miles from home, and there's no such thing as a taxi in this town."

Tod grinned into the falling snow. He had picked Dad's pocket. He had the car keys. It would be Miss Bartten who had to walk.

❧

Hiram Stratton, Jr., age twenty-one, had not known that anything could be worse than being locked in a small room with a Melancholia, a Deformity, a Conspiracy, and an Idiot.

But now it was he, Strat, who was the deformity.

He had let them attack Katie. Let them take it out on Douglass. He had groveled, reminding them that he was a good little boy, and could go out into the sunshine. And sure enough, here he was, in a special, iron-fenced garden he had never seen before, and sure enough the setting sun glittered on the deep white snow, the first thing of beauty he had seen in six months.

All the tiny offenses of his life were nothing to this. He breathed in the fine clear air for which he had sacrificed his soul.

It was not worth it.

Whether God forgave him or God did not, the forgiveness he needed now was Katie's, was Douglass's.

Strat no longer needed to worry how he, the victim, the patient, had gotten here; he needed to worry how he could stay a man in spite of being here.

There was Katie, whom God had seen fit to deliver into this world twisted and wrongly shaped, and people punished her for it.

There was Douglass, whom God had seen fit to deliver into this world without intelligence, and people punished him for it.

Poor Melancholia, who ached with depression, was punished for his grief. As for Conspiracy, she believed her family had locked her up to get her money. Strat would have believed her, because look what *his* family had done to *him*, except that her stories were never the same; were not stories even, but mad ravings.

Oh, Anna Sophia! thought Strat. You thought I possessed every virtue. You told me you would never meet a finer man. How wrong you were. I have never been a worse one.

In the beautiful snow garden, under the lengthening blue shadows, Strat, too, was in pain. *What have I done? I have not helped Katie or Douglass. I am a person to be ashamed of.*

"May I go back to my room now?" he said quietly to Ralph.

Devonny Aurelia Victoria Stratton and Walker Walkley moved slowly toward Fifth Avenue. Each elegant house —French mansard, Italianate, Gothic Revival—had bulbous stairs leading steeply up to a high first floor, and from each, the snow was constantly swept, lest a lady or gentleman slip.

The party was not far: one of the Vanderbilt houses on Fifth Avenue. It was a good-bye party for Devonny herself, because she would leave for California in the morning, and her father had not told her when she would return to New York. Father and her stepmother, Florinda, had gone to California on a whim, and found it surprisingly warm and gracious. (This was Florinda's word—her father would not know what gracious was if he lived another fifty years.)

Walker Walkley was tall and dramatic in his beaver coat and top hat. Walk saluted another gentleman with his cane. "Good evening," they said back and forth, bowing and nodding.

Devonny was grateful for her hooded cape of sea otter, lined with wine-red velvet. She needed it against the terrible cold.

Pinkerton detectives hired by the Vanderbilts scattered the homeless and the beggars, which was good, because their presence ruined a party. And one never knew, there might be criminals or anarchists among them. Gangs were trying to take over the streets of New York.

And then, beyond Walker Walkley, Devonny saw something that even Pinkerton detectives would not know what to do about.

Miss Lockwood.

Lurching through the snow, peering, staring . . . lost.

Her clothes were ridiculous, frozen into pathetic shapes. Of course she had no hat, and her hair hung like an immigrant's from Ellis Island. I expect *her* to rescue *us?* thought Devonny.

And now the foolish girl was about to ask Walker himself for directions! Walker would recognize her! That must never, never happen, Walker was too dangerous. Any hope would be ruined.

Devonny stood tiptoe, making herself as tall as she could, hoping her cheeks were pink and romantic from the cold. She brought those cheeks very close to Walk's. "Walk, I have been hard of heart because of Strat." She managed to let her hood slip, so that her hair was fetchingly free in the romantic snow. "But I have had many long talks with the minister's wife and she has helped me understand how very, very kind you were to intervene in a desperate situation."

Walk looked startled, as well he might. Devonny never went to church if she could avoid it, and certainly never discussed anything with the minister's wife, who was a fool and a shrew. But this was the best Devonny could manage under pressure. Devonny withdrew one hand from her muff and gently stroked Walk's cheek. The intimacy of this gesture shocked him; shocked Devonny too. She felt as if she were stroking the devil.

"After all," said Devonny sadly and loudly, "when a young man loses his mind, and cannot speak intelligibly, and cannot think clearly, it is the duty of his closest friend to act swiftly. I see now that it was quite wonderful of you to find Evergreen Asylum and help Father bring Strat there for treatment."

Walk recovered quickly. It was one of his best skills. He smiled. "All is forgiven, Devonny my dear. Of course we cherished Strat, but lunacy must be taken off the streets and away from loved ones. I am confident the doctors will find a way to bring Strat back from his insanity."

You're hoping he dies first, thought Devonny. She tucked herself against Walk's heavy coat. Luckily beaver was so thick she could feel nothing of the man himself. Otherwise she would have become quite faint. "It will be a great relief to me to leave in the morning. The train trip to the West Coast will restore me. You were so clever to convince Father that what I need is to be in California with him and Florinda and not here in New York, sitting alone and worried at Number Forty-four, fretting about my poor unfortunate brother. Thank you, Walker."

Well, she just hoped Miss Lockwood was listening. This was for her benefit and if Anna Sophia Lockwood was not paying attention, they were both in trouble, because Devonny could hardly run through her instructions again.

Devonny dared not look up from her position. She

just had to pray that the pedestrian who swept behind them was Anna Sophia Lockwood.

"Your brother . . . ," said Walker Walkley.

If she had to listen to Walker talk about Strat, Devonny might just seize Walk's cane and ram it down his throat in revenge. "Flossie and I went to the Museum this afternoon, Walk," she said. "How I wish you had been with us. I do adore mummies. I want to go to Egypt shortly. I've shopped in Paris and seen theater in London and that's enough of that. I think a cruise on the Nile would be just right. I want to dig among the pyramids. I feel I am destined to find an important mummy of my own."

Actually Devonny would have liked to embalm Walker, and turn him into a mummy.

While her tongue rambled, her mind got sharp. Like her father, Devonny had always been able to think of several things at once. When she was little, Father had taken her often to his office. She had run around filling the inkwells, while people beamed at her. Little girls are so amusing when they play Office. But young ladies are not. Young ladies must be kept at home and taught to play Wife.

Devonny intended to be an excellent wife but she felt she could also run an excellent office. Right now she was going to run a superior rescue.

Somehow she would whip Miss Lockwood into shape. It did not look, from her brief glimpse in the dark, as if there were much to work with, but Anna Sophia Lockwood was all Devonny had. She would send Miss Lockwood to the insane aylum. This would prove that Strat had not made the girl up. Strat would then be released.

Devonny worried for a moment that the Asylum might keep Miss Lockwood instead, because what sane person would behave as she had? But Evergreen was a private asylum and cost a great deal of money, and her father was unlikely to pay the bill for Miss Lockwood. So that was fine, then, and soon Strat would be out and of course would rush to Harriett's side, and Harriett would be restored by love and get completely well, and everybody would live happily ever after.

It was a fine plan.

Devonny swept into the Vanderbilt Mansion as if it were her own. She was stunning in her peach brocade gown, with its intricate layers of lace and its careful stitching to show off her tiny waist. Naturally Devonny had eaten a cracker beforehand, so she would not feel hunger. Having food tonight was out of the question. Chewing was not pretty.

"Gussie!" she cried, kissing a friend. "Mildred! Alice!" Devonny kissed busily in circles, even people she disliked or had hoped would move to Philadelphia. Quickly she had lots of space between herself and Walker Walkley.

Her mind flew.

Miss Lockwood would need money. This was difficult. Devonny did not often have access to cash. Miss Lockwood would need a wardrobe. This was difficult too. Devonny's things were packed for the great journey, some already shipped, much else in trunks and valises and hatboxes. Miss Lockwood would need directions. Devonny did not precisely know where Evergreen was. Miss Lockwood would have to be resourceful.

The real looming problem was that Miss Lockwood's century was an ill-mannered place where ladies behaved improperly and wore horrifying pieces of cloth instead of fashion.

Devonny hoped that Anna Sophia would be an eager learner when it came to dress. Surely she would want to cast off those street-urchin rags.

Walker Walkley cut through the press of ladies, and there was no doubt from his stride that he meant to repossess Devonny.

Walker Walkley actually living in *her* town house! Disgusting! How dare Father treat Walk like a son? How dare Father take Walk's word for things instead of Strat's?

Devonny felt herself turning into her father, a ferocious human being, who, if the whiskey or claret did not suit him, would stomp his huge boot on the floor until the servants came running and improved themselves. Her features turned hard as a railroad baron's as she thought what she would like to do right now.

But Walk must suspect nothing. His whole mind must be consumed with rapture for Devonny.

She let her strong shoulders sag. She opened her rosebud mouth to soften her lips, lowered her long lashes and fluttered her wrists. She trembled so he would see his dominance.

It was a dance of sorts. He danced with strength. She danced with weakness.

But I will win, thought Devonny Aurelia Victoria Stratton. In the end, Walker Walkley, I will make an Egyptian mummy out of you.

✐ CHAPTER 3 ✐

Strat stumbled after Ralph, his feet bumbling around as if he didn't ordinarily walk. And of course, for several months, he hadn't ordinarily walked. Ralph, too, was bumbling along. He was smiling, because Strat, whipped and beaten, had asked to be jailed once more. But he was not looking. What was there to look at?

Every fiber of Strat awoke.

Every molecule of energy raced to the surface. His apathetic soul leaped toward the most important thing: *escape.*

Evergreen was no remodeled mansion where difficult people had bedrooms. It had been constructed to store the insane. Its walls were thick stone, its windows high and narrow. Its doors were heavy with keyed locks, and the keys hung from brass circles which attendants like Ralph strapped through their belts.

Beyond the buildings were very high, iron grille

fences, and twenty yards beyond those, walls of mortared stone in which glass shards were imbedded.

Every guard carried something to hit with: flat sticks, circular bats, linked steel balls. Ralph was armed with a club.

When they passed from the snow garden into the building, Ralph actually held the door for Strat. Strat slammed the door into the attendant's face and knocked him out in a shower of blood. Strat stepped quickly back outside and surveyed the obstacles between himself and freedom.

Snow was in his favor.

Shoveled by trusted inmates against the iron fences, it was packed high enough for a three- or four-foot boost. Strat could easily grasp the top horizontal bar and swing himself over onto the white expanse. Then the only problem would be the glass-studded wall.

So he would cut himself. What were cuts in the hand compared to freedom?

Even as he ran, even as he found to his joy that the snow *would* hold him and his hands *did* have strength and he *could* vault over the eight-foot fence, he was planning his future.

He would never go home. What was there for him? A mother who had not come, a fiancée who had not written, a sister who had not visited, and a father who had chosen this.

No. He was going into the wilderness. He would vanish forever and build a new life, a manly life.

Not in America. It had no more wilderness, it was boring, there was no more Wild West. Alaska was a possibility, and of course Africa. The source of the Nile had been discovered, but surely there was something left for Strat to do.

Thinking of the Nile, of crocodiles and pyramids, Strat slogged through white drifts. It was slow going. The narrow windows of Evergreen had advantages. Even those who were allowed to look out rarely did.

He reached the stone wall. His bare fingers scrabbled against the jutting rocks, gripping a one-inch protrusion here and a half-inch ledge there. The cold he did not notice. When he hoisted himself up, supporting himself by shoving his toes in cracks supplied by the stonemason, he discovered that the glass was in a neat, straight line, and he could avoid it without the slightest difficulty.

Laughing, Strat tipped himself over, landing in a snowdrift, not getting a single bruise.

He had escaped.

❧

Number Forty-four, thought Annie, and saw the immense building right away.

The town house looked as if several architects had owned their own quarries and each man had thrown his own stone at the walls and steps. Brownstone, limestone, granite and marble. Above that, stained glass and wrought iron.

Annie had known the Strattons were well-to-do, but she had not realized that their beach mansion was a simple summer cottage. A throwaway. Here was the real wealth and the real Mansion.

45

Devonny and Walker Walkley disappeared into the snow. Oh, Strat! thought Annie. I'm doing this for you, *and you're not here!*

She tried to cling to the memory of Strat, but there was nothing to cling to here, nothing at all.

High frightening steps climbed steeply to an immense front door. There was no comfy porch. Either the doorman admitted a caller promptly, or there was a risk of falling backward onto the distant sidewalk.

Annie knocked on Number Forty-four.

The door opened. Electric light from cute little pointy bulbs illuminated a huge hall. Hideous wallpaper shrieked at her. Immense oil portraits of frightening ancestors, a stag's head with sprawling antlers, and an enormous glass display stuffed with dead pheasants crowded the walls.

Annie dripped onto the carpet.

Two people regarded her with suspicion. The man wore a tailcoat, a high starched white collar and a fat black bow tie; the woman had on a floor-length black gown with a shiny black overdress. They looked like people on their way to a fashionable evening funeral, but she was pretty sure they were just servants, and the shiny overdress was actually an apron.

Frozen, slush-covered and torn, Annie tried to think of a way to make these people keep her. Or at least warm her up. "Good evening," said Annie. Her mind was time-sloshed. Strat, suffering loss of mind and thought? Strat, in an insane asylum? "I am Miss Anna Sophia Lockwood," she managed at last. "I am a very dear friend of Miss Devonny's from Connecticut. A dreadful thing has occurred. I most desperately require your aid."

The man was already taking her black coat, shaking off the snow and brushing it down with his gloved hand. "What is that, Miss Lockwood?" he said sympathetically.

What is that? wondered Annie. "I was robbed!" she improvised. "Some dreadful individual, some wicked man!"

"Oh, miss, how awful!" cried the maid, accepting her story right away. "The streets is full of such these days. No matter what the hour, criminals and gangs wander those sidewalks."

They escorted her into an immense, amazing room. The ceilings soared so high Annie felt as if she were in Grand Central Station again. Indigo-blue skies were painted with gold-leaf stars and crescent moons and suns with trembling rays. Layers of rugs covered the floors, and collections—Chinese bronze here, Tiffany glass there—were distributed as casually as schoolbooks.

Every piece of furniture was rounded: drawers on magnificent desks bowed outward and sides of enormous arm chairs puffed and heaved. Everything that could have gold on it did. Gold mirror frames, gold umbrella stands, gold feet on fern stands and gold statues and gold braid festooned on gold-threaded curtains.

"Are you all right, miss?" asked the butler anxiously. "Did he hurt you?"

"No," said Annie quickly, lest they send the police

looking for her fictional attacker. "But he took my reticule. I have no money and no ticket for the train home." Annie was rather pleased with the word *reticule,* but the maid looked confused. Perhaps Annie was wrong about what they called a purse. Oh, well. Moving right along, she thought. "I'm soaked," she said. "I must have a hot bath." She counted on being beautiful to carry her through. Beauty was useful in life. People thought it said things about you, and now she wanted these two servants to think it said, *You want me for a houseguest. I am the sort of houseguest you usually have.* "Miss Devonny will be delighted to let me stay the night," she assured them, "and now I am simply too weary to go on. You must get me dry clothing. Hers will fit me; we often exchange gowns when Miss Devonny visits me in Connecticut."

The servants were used to obeying and believing. Annie was whisked up the front stairs into a charming guest room while a bath was quickly drawn. Tall radiators against the walls clacked and bonged as hot water boiled through them. The bedroom was stifling. It had to be eighty degrees, the air stale with old perfume.

"What's your name?" she asked the maid.

"Schmidt."

Annie made her first error of the century by requesting Schmidt to open the windows. "It's so stuffy, Schmidt."

It was not windows but Schmidt's mouth that opened, in amazement. "We don't open windows, miss. You mustn't let in night air. Surely you don't open your windows out there in the country! Why, you have

48

swamps and marshes and all manner of unhealthy air out there." The horror of night air upset Schmidt so much that she unloosened vast, heavy draperies and yanked them shut over the offending sight of windows.

Schmidt undressed her for the bath, appalled at the lack of decent undergarments. No corset, no chemise, no long drawers, no woolen stockings. Annie's lovely blue knit dress Schmidt treated as an appalling rag, and held it with her fingertips. "It's ruined!" cried Annie. "That dreadful man ripped off all the ribbons and all the lace and all the—I can't talk about it."

Schmidt felt much better about the gown now that she knew the good parts had been torn off.

"I'll just rest in the hot water for a while," said Annie, hoping Schmidt would leave. But Schmidt sat on a three-legged stool next to the tub as if she were going to play the piano. It was difficult to have a witness. It made for a short, efficient bath. Annie was tucked into a bed so occupied by pillows there was hardly room to lie down.

A knock on the door was supper on a footed tray. The tray was beautiful. A tiny brass railing kept crystal glasses from slipping off. A frail bone-china cup held tea. There was a bowl of thick creamy soup and a funny little white pudding decorated with colored sugar fruit that Annie associated with inedible Christmas cakes. Annie sipped the dark red liquid in the smallest glass and nearly gagged. It was thick as syrup and absolutely disgusting. Was it medicine?

"The best claret, miss, good for chills.

"Lovely," said Annie. "Thank you so much.

took no more risks, and sipped tea. It tasted as if it had been brewing since it left India. "I was so fond of young Mr. Stratton, Schmidt. I know the dreadful course of action that was taken. Please tell me how he is doing now. Is he all right?"

"Oh, miss, it's such a shame. His poor mother has tried to visit, but Mr. Stratton's instructions are no visitors. Poor lady sold her jewelry to get the train ticket, went all the way up north, and was not permitted in. But she said the Evergreen place was beautiful, and they reassured her that he is receiving the very best of treatment." Schmidt tended to the pillows, fluffing and rearranging.

Annie could not eat. She could only cry.

"Now, miss," said the maid comfortingly, "he's in the best of care. These asylums as they have for gentlemen, they're not like the state asylums."

Asylum. It conjured up cold gray stones and thin lumpy mattresses: crazy people screaming through the night.

She felt stalled, ruined. How was she supposed to cope with insanity? She hadn't brought tranquilizers. She had never counseled anybody in her life, just gossiped with her girlfriends.

Did I do it? she thought. *Did falling in love with a girl who fell through Time send him over an edge of his own? Oh, Time. Did you bring me back to make me look at what a vicious thing I did, interrupting their lives?* "And Miss Harriett?" asked Annie, sick with worry.

The maid drooped. "Bleeding of the lungs. Of course she couldn't stay here and make everybody else sick. They looked in the Blue Ridge Mountains for better air, but the towns there don't take lungsick. It ruins a town's looks, you know, to have all those thin, dying people around. Up in the Adirondacks, though, it used to be just for hunting and fishing and men who like that kind of thing, getting wet in their canoes and making campfires, but now of course it's for cure cottages, and I understand the mountain air cleans out the lungs." Schmidt took away the tray. "Sometimes, anyway," she added, striving to be precise. "Mostly they die."

Time, you monster! Why didn't you tell me to bring medicine? You brought me here to see the end of Strat and Harriett both?

I'm a lunatic myself, Annie realized. Look at me, addressing Time as if he exists and he's the bad guy.

Annie told the maid to let her sleep. "When Miss Devonny and Mr. Walk come in, Schmidt, please don't tell Mr. Walkley I'm here." How to keep him out of the picture? Walker Walkley had been rotten then and no doubt he was rotten now, or Devonny would not have kept his eyes cupped in her hands to prevent him from seeing Annie.

Possibly a half-truth would do. The sort they used in this century. "Once Mr. Walkley was forward with me," she murmured, "and I am uncomfortable in his company."

"I'll be ever so careful, miss, don't you worry."

51

Don't worry? thought Annie Lockwood. I changed Time to find Strat, and he's hundreds of miles away, locked in an asylum, and Devonny is dating Walk, who put him there?

On the bedside table was a lovely little calendar, painted by hand with cherubs and roses. February, it said. 1898, it said.

"1898?" she cried.

Schmidt stared at her.

"I mean, I'm really so tired, Schmidt," said Annie, who felt herself unraveling like an old towel, "you are so good to me, thank you so much." Only nine months passed in my century. How could three years have passed here? What is Time doing?

"Shall I sit with you until you are asleep, miss?" asked Schmidt, and Annie thought of her mother, who sat with Annie or Tod whenever they didn't feel well so they'd have company for falling asleep.

What is it about sleep that makes us afraid to fall alone? Where have I fallen . . . alone?

❧

In the shanties north of Central Park, immigrants shuddered with cold and postponed as long as possible a trip to the outhouse.

But at the Vanderbilts', guests dined among real grape arbors, brought at great expense from southern greenhouses. At each place, tucked among fresh flowers rushed north by train, were gifts. The men received engraved silver boxes, whose round lids hinged up to take wooden matchsticks for lighting cigars; the ladies were given crystal perfume bottles, their stoppers encrusted with diamonds.

The soups were duck and turtle, the dinner was roast mountain sheep with puree of chestnuts, and wines of superior vintage accompanied the meal. An opera singer and her orchestra entertained.

Walker Walkley regarded opera as a series of Indian war whoops, and he would have preferred the Indians.

During the boring recital, he looked with approval at Devonny's friend Flossie. How refined she was! So thin that she literally could not support herself, but must lean upon her escort. Naturally Flossie hardly looked up and hardly spoke, and it was so beautiful, such weakness. This was how women should be.

Devonny, whose behavior could be quite unbecoming, went horseback riding every day when the weather was good and ice skating when it was not. After their marriage, he would put a stop to it. Walk would keep her in the house for a year, no exercise and no sun, because the girl was practically *brown* from being outdoors, and because restraint would calm her down.

When Devonny smiled at him, the usual surge of desire swept over Walk. He—he alone—was going to have that Stratton money. And if he could engineer it, he would also have Harriett Ranleigh's money.

Walk liked the finer things in life. He did not have enough of them. Soon that would change.

He smiled back at Devonny, but of course did not cease his conversation with Mr. Astor. Whatever it was that Devonny wanted to say would keep. (Anything any woman wanted to say would keep.)

Walk was content, thinking of putting Devonny where she belonged.

All day Harriett had been beautiful. Fever brushed her pink, accented her pallor and made her lovely.

The same fever had delivered night sweats so bad the entire bed was soaked and had to be changed in the dark. How could there be any liquid left in her? She was going to dry out and die a crisp little wafer.

"Now, dear," said Moss, "let's have a smile on that beautiful face, and then a glass of milk."

Six glasses of milk had to be swallowed every day. Harriett hated anything to do with cows now. "When I am well, I will go to the South Seas and eat mangos," she said to Moss.

Moss's assistant, Mario, a skinny boy who carried, emptied and lifted, changed her again. Consumption was a filthy disease. Nobody talked about that. It was important not to refer to the actual squalor of the sickroom. It was important to maintain the fiction that one died gently, setting an example, and going willingly to God.

But coughing hurt so much. Her whole body hurt. For the first time, Harriett was willing to give up her body. It was too hard to live in it.

I am so afraid, thought Harriett. And so cold.

Devonny had soaked her pillows many nights with her tears and fears. She had wept for her dearest friend, Harriett, whose decline had turned out to be consumption, and for her beloved brother, Strat, when Father turned against him. Now she soaked the pillows in her bedroom with tears of rage and frustration.

One of the problems here was that just because Father was in California did not mean that Father was out of reach.

In this dreadful new world, people were never out of reach. There were telephones and telegraphs. It was hideous. You could have Father on the opposite coast of America—*with thousands of miles in between*—and still, bad people like Walker Walkley could get in touch with him *that very day*.

Walker Walkley came into everything.

Suddenly Devonny realized that it was Walk who had taken the mail to the post each morning. The footman had always done it, but Walker insisted that he needed the exercise.

He didn't mail our letters, thought Devonny. Strat does not know we've been writing. Maybe even Harriett does not know we've been writing. Maybe they are both alone, without knowing they are loved and missed. All my letters of encouragement . . . they were never mailed.

Forget mummies. Devonny wanted Walker Walkley to kneel down with Marie Antoinette. A guillotine would improve him.

Exhausted from the party and the constant need to be helpless and clinging, Devonny was now far too close to sleep. Sleep would be a grave error. Devonny got out of bed and paced the hot room to keep herself awake.

Walk simply would not go to bed. What was the matter with that man? He was down there in Father's smoking room, striding back and forth as if he owned it.

Walker Walkley, you toad. It's good I'm going to California. I will find somebody to marry. Anybody. Anybody at all. As long as he's tall and handsome, of course, and speaks beautifully and is educated and well traveled. I'll marry him quickly and that will serve Walker Walkley right.

Her vision of California was wonderfully sunny, full of orange and palm groves, and rows of flawless men to whom she would be introduced.

Meantime, there was work to be done.

She ran her mind over the battalion of servants in the house. Naturally one didn't know them personally, and after the Lockwood problem at the summer cottage, Father had dismissed everybody and replaced them with strangers.

Devonny was going to have to entrust one or more of these strangers with the safety of Anna Sophia.

It would have to be Schmidt. Devonny was not fond of Schmidt, who talked steadily and boringly, but the woman had already let Miss Lockwood in and given her a bath, and unless Miss Lockwood had improved, Schmidt had probably already learned secrets a servant should not possess.

It was two in the morning.

Schmidt had gone to bed.

Devonny was annoyed. Servants had minds of their own these days. Father was right. A person had to be strict with them.

She buzzed Schmidt.

∾⧳⧳

Katie had known, of course, that the truly insane at Evergreen were the attendants: men and women who loved to hit. Violence was constant. They would kick a person over any excuse or none. With those heavy key rings they liked to hit patients in the face. They told Katie they didn't hit her in the face because she was so ugly the scars wouldn't show. They struck her hands instead.

Poor Strat.

If he had been poor all his life, perhaps he could have completed his escape. But he had behaved like a rich man, expecting to be welcomed at an inn in the village and given a room with a hot bath. The innkeeper simply summoned the staff from the asylum.

Strat had fought, and now had no chance whatever of getting out of Evergreen. He truly was dangerous. He had broken a man's arm and knocked a tooth from another man's jaw, and as for Ralph, Ralph's head still rang from the collision of that door against his nose and eye sockets, and Ralph was not a forgiving person.

They put Strat in the straitjacket: a canvas shirt whose arms were mittened at the tips, with straps that tied Strat's arms to his chest. Then he was given treatment. The treatment consisted of reducing him to a mass of bruises.

From the only kind attendant at Evergreen, Katie obtained a cup of warm water and a relatively clean cloth. She bathed Strat's wounds when Ralph finally quit, and talked to Strat constantly, to keep him calm. When he swore or talked back, they simply hit him again. It was a very long night. Actually, it could have been day by now; Katie had no window and no sun by which to gauge.

"Katie," said Strat, through swollen painful lips, "why? Why doesn't even my mother come?"

Katie began working the knots out of his hair. She felt that Strat could not go on if he believed his mother did not love him, so she said, "Your dear mother loves you, but has never been told where you are. I expect your dear sister loves you, but has also been kept unaware. Or else they truly believe you are in some pleasant place receiving kind treatment."

Katie, who had never received kindness, knew how to give it.

"If they'd just let me out!" cried Strat.

Since they were not going to let him out, Katie continued to say nothing on that subject. She felt terribly sorry for him. It was easier for her, because she had not known much else.

"Katie, if you could get out," asked Strat, "where would you go?"

Katie did not laugh bitterly. She simply heard his question. "I have nowhere to go. I am deformed. I will always be deformed. No one would want me."

Douglass snuffled, making his "read to me" sound. Katie picked up her Bible and read.

"They'd have put Jesus in an insane asylum," said Strat.

"No, said Katie, "because he was beautiful. And so were his disciples. To be ugly is the worst thing. Nobody forgives you for that."

～ჯ

"We have very little time," said Devonny, giving the sleeping Miss Lockwood a rough shake, "and we must accomplish a thousand things before Walk appears in the morning. Noon, actually. He's never up before noon."

Annie struggled to wake up. She had centuries to cross and bad dreams to throw off.

"First of all," said Devonny Stratton to Annie Lockwood, "I want you to admit that this is All. Your. Fault."

∽ CHAPTER 4 ∼

Annie wished she were a hundred years later, safe in her own time, when people let you use any excuse at all. You never had to be responsible for what you did, because it could always be somebody else's fault.

"Listen to me, Miss Lockwood," said Devonny Stratton sharply. She did not look forgiving. "Because he wept for you—because he wrote an essay at Yale describing your century—because he wandered around the mansion grounds calling for you and looking behind trees for you—my brother looked insane."

How could such a perfect love have such a horrible result?

Oh, no, thought Annie, please no! It was true love, not insanity.

"Walker Walkley," said Devonny, as harsh as winter,

"found out about that essay and weaseled himself back into our lives, telling lies and more lies and greater lies to Father. Father believed him, and the ministers at Yale thought that Strat was godless and . . . well, it's all your fault, Miss Lockwood. My brother is not insane. But knowing you made him appear insane."

If only the lights were not on. In soft, cozy dark this would not sound so horrible. If she were under the covers it would sound like a scary bedtime story, not a death sentence.

"Everything *is* my fault," said Annie. Her heart wrenched apart, separated chambers beating against each other. It hurt terribly.

Such a beautiful room for such a confrontation. And even in the middle of the night, all three women were beautifully clothed: voluminous white gowns, with lace and ruffles and embroidered flowers. In contrast to daytime, they wore their hair down: Devonny's actually reached her waist, and Schmidt's reached below hers. Schmidt's was streaked with gray and Devonny's with gold. Even their hair said who they were in life, and what they owned.

Annie's hair, which once Strat had threaded through his fingers and made into horsetails, lay straight and dark on her shoulders. "I'm sorry," she whispered. "I didn't go through Time on purpose. I didn't choose your family. Time chose you."

Schmidt was gaping at them. High and broad in her heavy nightgown, she looked like an overweight Statue of Liberty.

"However, Anna Sophia . . . ," said Devonny. Her voice cracked. She was only a teenager herself, no older than Annie. (Annie was so completely her name: Anna Sophia felt like somebody else.)

Devonny soldiered on. "In spite of the terrible things you did to us, Anna Sophia, we loved you."

They loved me, she thought. And I loved them. But I loved Strat the most. Strat, what have I done to you? How can I make up for it?

"Even Harriett loved you," said Devonny, "and you were such a threat to her future."

Does Harriett even have a future now? thought Annie. Surely they can't blame me that she got sick.

"But now," said Devonny, "now you must prove your worth, Miss Lockwood."

Prove her worth?

Right.

Annie wasn't worth anything even to her own father.

How glad she was to be lying among soft pillows. You could count on pillows to comfort you, even when everybody in your life turned against you. Annie hugged a pillow.

"Repack the trunks, Schmidt," said Devonny, stabbing a finger toward the proper clothing. "Silently. Nobody must hear a sound from this room. Miss Lockwood is heading north. Find warm things for her. She must be stylish. Fashion will be important. She must impress people in order to get my brother out of Evergreen."

Oh, good, thought Annie. I get to live.

Schmidt chose a trunk so large you could carry a

bodyguard in it, or enough clothing to last a generation.

"Schmidt will order a cab to take you to the Hudson Nightline Pier, whence you will take a steamboat to Albany. From thence, the Delaware and Hudson train, disembarking at Evergreen, New York. This is the site of the asylum to which my brother has been confined. I do not know the exact address, but I presume the natives keep track of their lunatic asylums and will guide you."

Annie was stunned. Devonny was sending her out into some wilderness to a lunatic asylum? "But Devonny, how can I possibly do that?"

"You'll behave yourself like a proper lady. You won't talk to people," explained Devonny. "It isn't ladylike to address strangers. But you'll use feminine wiles, of course."

"No, Devonny, you have to go with me!"

"I cannot. Walker Walkley reports to Father. Walk will put me on the train to California tomorrow and I must take it. If I don't, he will know something is happening and he will stop it. You must be very careful of Walker Walkley, Miss Lockwood. He will stop at nothing. There is so much money at stake."

"What do you mean, he will stop at nothing?" said Annie. "Do you mean he's a murderer or a kidnapper?"

"He's a kidnapper anyway. How do you think they got Strat to an asylum? They tricked him and kidnapped him."

Annie flopped back on the pillows as if she were Raggedy Ann.

Schmidt filled a hat box: towering impossible hats, with built-in neck scarves and posturing feathers and hanging beads.

Fashion is supposed to get me in there? Annie wondered about this theory. I'm supposed to use a hat to break down locks?

"You must address the situation there," said Devonny, kneeling on the bed. "I do not know what Father has set up." Devonny bounced angrily. "Your job is to make it clear to the authorities that my brother is *not* a lunatic! You must substantiate that *you exist.*"

Schmidt, folding gowns, paused.

"This is not your affair, Schmidt," said Devonny severely.

"Yes, miss," said Schmidt.

It seemed to Annie that Schmidt was packing an excess of nightgowns and not enough morning, afternoon, and evening gowns, but if she were overhearing this conversation, her packing skills might be off too. "What if they don't believe me, Devonny? I'm a good liar, and I've had lots of practice lately, but what if I don't pull it off?"

"Then you will have to take Strat with you into your own Time. I have given this a great deal of thought, Anna Sophia. What matters is my brother."

Take Strat back into her own Time.

What an astonishing thought. Whisk him over the decades, holding his hand as they fell up a century. There he would be—handsome, funny, sweet strong Strat.

And then what? Annie couldn't manage a father and mother, or friends, or school trips, or even a purse. She was too dizzy to move Strat to the twentieth century. And yet . . . how lovely it would be.

"Devonny, wait a minute. You expect me to take on lunatic asylums and buy train tickets and carry my own trunk? Look at the size of that thing. I'd need a squad just to carry it."

"That's what porters are for," said Devonny irritably. "You pay people to carry your trunk." Devonny grabbed her shoulders. "Listen. You started this and you have to finish it. I have not been able to leave the house without Walker Walkley escorting me! I have not been able to mail my own letters. Our mother, because Father divorced her, of course has no standing and can accomplish nothing. She had to sell a brooch in order to get money to travel to Evergreen, and then they would not break Father's instructions just for a woman! They never let her see her son."

"I'm a woman too," said Annie feebly. Where were the gala balls and fine gowns? She did not want responsibility! There was enough of that in other centuries. In this century, a woman was supposed to be sheltered and entertained.

"I have been sent for," said Devonny harshly. "Father is requiring me to come to California. I can make no choices. But *you* are different. You told us so. You said in your century you make the choices. We're counting on you."

Annie hated being quoted at awkward times. I'll

choose to go home after all, she thought. This won't be a romantic adventure. Strat isn't even here! In every way, this will be dark and icy and slippery.

"You said women can do anything," Devonny told her.

Annie flushed. She probably had said that. She had probably even believed it. But surely, when you changed centuries, you got to change burdens. Is that why I came? she thought. So it would be easier?

Schmidt, who was not supposed to be listening, said, "I came from Germany, miss. I did not speak English. I learned how to get here and how to get a job. So you can learn how to get up the Hudson River."

Immigrants were always boasting about how hard they had struggled. In her own time, men rowed in leaky rafts across shark-infested waters in order to leave Haiti and find jobs in America and take better care of their families—and she, Annie Lockwood, wouldn't even take a cab across Manhattan?

"Thank you, Schmidt," said Devonny when she saw that Annie was conquered. "You shall be rewarded." This was as much attention as she gave a maid, however. "You'll need money, Anna Sophia. I have taken everything I can find. Actually the only person with cash is Walker, so I have appropriated his. He owes it to me, anyway."

Devonny had appropriated Walk's cash? What did that mean? Had she lifted his wallet? Emptied his checking account? Or wherever people kept their dollars in 1898? But that was stealing. Annie was supposed to spend those stolen dollars? Belonging to a man who had already kidnapped and Devonny thought would murder too?

Annie said anxiously, "What if he has some household servant arrested for it? What if he suspects"— Annie tried not to look at Schmidt—"one of your maids or something?"

"These things happen," said Devonny, who, indeed, was very like her father. "Now, for Harriett. She has consumption. I know that she can be cured by true love. I absolutely know this. So once you get Strat out, you must journey onward to Clear Pond."

"Is that in the Adirondacks too?"

"Everything is. Mountain air is of use both to the insane and to the consumptive. Questions?"

Annie would like to have taken Devonny back to the twentieth century with her and have Devonny straighten Miss Bartten out. But the words that came from Annie's mouth were nineteenth-century words. "I shall not let you down," she said firmly. The words resounded in the Victorian bedroom, and Annie was proud.

"Good," said Devonny. "Schmidt, it is practically dawn. Let's get her dressed."

❧

It was morning in the Adirondacks too.

Harriett was awestruck by the beauty of new-fallen snow. Everything was a choir robe, a child in a Christmas play. All dark branches of all dark trees bowed down with snow in their arms.

And indeed, the sounds of children could be heard.

67

In this silent isolation, a family had come to visit! They had come by sleigh, the snow and the sable furs all part of a great adventure.

I would find it a great adventure, too, thought Harriett, if it had what all adventure requires—going home again.

Children dashed through the snow, whooping and hollering.

How wonderful their voices sounded to Harriett.

When I die, she thought, will I hear the voices of children again? It takes such courage to stay here. It is so awful, so dull, so cold, so alone. We try to bolster each other, but it is hard. We patients want two things.

To be well.

To be home.

And I . . . I want a third.

Strat.

❧

Tod Lockwood knocked on his sister's bedroom door.

Nobody answered.

It had that complete dusty silence of when nobody is there.

Slowly, Tod opened Annie's door.

Nobody was there.

He didn't want to think about it. The other times— those two terrifying, maddening times when she had gone off by herself—the community and the police searching for her—Mom and Dad nuts with worry— himself realizing that he actually loved his sister . . .

Well, she had done it again.

And Tod Lockwood did not love her for it.

"Fine," he said to the silent room. "Be rotten. See if I care."

He slammed the door and stomped out of the house to school.

He wouldn't cover her tracks for her because he had no idea where her tracks were. She had covered them pretty darn well the other times.

But he wouldn't tell on her either.

He wouldn't let Mom in Japan worry and he wouldn't allow Dad back into the family he'd deserted.

So there.

"How intriguing!" cried Beanie.

The peddler beamed from beneath his mustache.

"You're not going to buy one, are you, Beanie?" said Harriett disapprovingly.

"Harriett, darling, I'll try anything." Beanie fitted the glass helmet over her head. It didn't go. She had to take off her earmuffs and scarf. Now it fit. Harriett giggled, looking at her.

"What on earth?" demanded Moss the nurse. "Take that monstrosity away from your face immediately, Miss Beatrice."

"It's a re-breather, Moss," said Beanie. From behind the glass bowl, her voice was muffled. Her breath fogged the glass and it was so cold on the porch Harriett expected the glass to frost.

"I beg your pardon," said Moss, more frostily than the weather. "The point of the cure is to breathe fresh mountain air."

"Ah ha!" cried the peddler. "Except if it's not working. And then the newest thing is to rebreathe your own used breath. Those special gases have healing properties."

"You are responsible for following all rules of the cure, Miss Beatrice!" said Moss. "I'm sure I cannot be responsible for what happens if you neglect the procedure."

Beanie rebreathed lustily.

Fundamental to cure were the rules. The slightest break might lead down the path of death instead of the path of life. Beanie's rebreather might remove the fragile barrier between herself and her Maker.

Charlie, having just left the billiards room, came slowly up the path, smoking his pipe, assisted by his man and two canes. Of course he wanted to try on the rebreathing apparatus.

Harriett distracted Moss. "Did you go to school, Moss?" asked Harriett.

"I finished eighth grade, Miss Harriett. Then I nursed my mother, who died of consumption, my father, who died of it, and then my aunt, and then I decided to be a nurse here."

"You're a wonderful nurse," said Harriett.

"Thank you," said Moss happily. "I have climbed quite a ladder."

Harriett thought it a very short ladder. But the ladders of women usually were. "How is Lucy Leora?"

Harriett asked. Lucy Leora had the cottage behind the fir trees and Moss often helped Lucy Leora's nurse.

"She died in the night, Miss Harriett," said Moss calmly.

Beanie and Charlie were not listening. They were giggling and wasting lung energy over the glass helmet. They did not know that Death had come in the night.

Moss bustled around, replacing Harriet's cooled-off foot warmer with a hot soapstone just off the stove. "Lucy Leora had a good easy death. In her sleep. You may thank God."

Harriett did not thank God. He was too mean. Lucy Leora had been sixteen.

Dear Lord, prayed Harriett (because even if He was mean and took sixteen-year-olds, He was all Harriett had), I am still betrothed to Strat. It still counts, I know it does. I still wear his ring, and if he has not written to tell me he loves me, at least he has not written to tell me he loves another! *I must get well,* and we *will* have children, and live happily ever after, I know we will!

❧

The traveling hat, which tied under her chin with broad wool streamers, had a wide black velvet brim and five garnet-red ostrich plumes. It gave Annie grace and dignity, explained Devonny. A swollen roll of veiling collected around the hat rim, waiting to be unwrapped. Annie had no intention of veiling her face. There was such a thing as going too far.

Her dress was a pale-gray velvet, difficult swollen

71

buttons streaming down the back, fastened not into holes but into silk loops. The lower twelve inches of the dress was skirted with moiré, which could be detached and cleaned if the street soiled the hemline. The dress ribbons were garnet to match the hat plumes.

Beneath the dress of course was a corset laced tight enough to break ribs, a chemise to cover her limbs, and wool stockings held up above her knees with killer elastic bands.

Her ankle-length coat was sleek dark mink. Her black gloves reached her elbows, and her mitt was mink inside and out. Annie figured the costume was a quick way to gain fifty pounds.

Schmidt did not even smuggle Annie out of the town house. "Mr. Walker's still in bed, miss," explained Schmidt. "He's fond of his brandy. It takes him time in the morning to open his eyes and he needs even more brandy to do that." Servants carried Devonny's trunk—now Annie's—down the stairs.

"But what if he comes out and sees me?" she hissed at Schmidt. "What will you say?"

"I'll say 'Good morning, sir.'"

I have to be that calm, thought Annie. I have to hold my chin high and my plumes high and my muff high, and say things like "Good morning, sir," and swirl away in a haughty ladylike fashion.

The butler ordered a taxi. To Annie, this meant a Yellow Cab. But of course, it was a horse-drawn taxi—without wheels.

"A sleigh!" cried Annie, laughing. *Bells on bobtail ring,*

making spirits bright, what fun it is to ride and sing a
sleighing song tonight. Oh jingle bells, jingle bells . . . !

And they did jingle.

The two horses were adorned with leather straps hung with jingle bells bigger than anything on a door wreath: fat silvery bells, a hundred to chorus and jangle.

Devonny had not come down to see her off. Devonny in fact had gone back to bed, and according to Schmidt was sleeping soundly. Annie did not think this was fair.

The driver and his two horses seemed interested in suicide. They trotted between horse-drawn omnibuses and wired trolleys. They whipped under elevated railroads and sped between the convergence of tracks lying on the street. They aimed at pedestrians. People swore at them in various languages and shook their fists and once threw something.

Annie could have used a seat belt. What with one hand steadying her plume tower and one hand gripping the sleigh rim, she was exhausted.

The stench of New York was amazing. Annie bet that a hundred thousand horses had plopped dung into the streets. The sleigh hit all of it.

There were homeless people. Annie could not look at them now any more than she could bear looking at them a hundred years later.

The buildings were magnificent, and yet there was a gaunt, spare coldness to the city that frightened her. She could not tell, because they flew so fast over the packed snow, whether it was the newness of the buildings that was frightening or her own newness. She was as weak and vulnerable as the greenest immigrant to step off the boat.

When they arrived at the pier, the steamboat was much larger than she had expected. Open and squat like an enormous ferry, it had two huge, factory-size smokestacks. Smoke billowed, thick with ash and soot. Real sparks flew. She could hear the steam engines, hear the boilers smacking with the metallic sounds of gears and grinding. What a fire trap, she thought. I'm getting on that?

The driver stopped.

She was ashamed of the trunk. It was so huge. And the hatbox and the valise—she could hardly manage that paper hatbox, what with staying erect under the weight of all this clothing.

But it was immediately clear that people did not travel light in 1898.

Mountains of luggage were piled at the gangplanks. One single family ahead of her had as much baggage as a 747 carries to Europe. Annie's trunk and bag looked paltry and forlorn. She began to fret that she would not have enough to wear after all.

Porters were everywhere, which was a good thing, considering how much work they had ahead of them. They wore fine uniforms, like Marine officers on parade.

Every woman was veiled, and they were smarter than Annie. The soot and filth of the coal engines were coating her like paint. She tugged the veil down after all, and tucked it into her coat the way the other women did.

She didn't have to figure out how to buy a ticket; her driver and the porter accomplished this. She did buy a Coke, which cost a nickel. It made her happy to buy a Coke in a glass bottle and pay five cents for it. But that was the only happy thing.

Don't speak to strangers, Devonny had said sharply. It isn't becoming behavior for a lady.

But they were all strangers. How was she to manage without a single person in the world on her team? She could not possibly do this without Devonny.

At least she had a great hat.

∼⩥⩤∽

It had taken Walker Walkley two whole years to convince Mr. Stratton senior that young Strat was crazy.

Solid intense labor. Paper proof. Stealing Strat's English essays at Yale. Seizing Strat's diary from his locked room. He'd had to add a few sentences here and there, incriminating sentences in careful Strat-style handwriting.

But Walk had won.

Mr. Stratton could not allow the Stratton fortune to go to somebody whose mind was not intact. The man had fought and slashed his way to the top—he would never give that hard-won money to somebody at the bottom. Somebody to be ashamed of.

Strat, in other words.

So Strat would have none, Devonny would have it all, and Walker Walkley would marry Devonny.

The plan was taking longer than Walk had thought, and Devonny had been more difficult, but he was close.

He awoke slowly to his hangover. It was past noon before he could actually open his swollen eyelids. Following Mr. Stratton's example, Walk banged hard on the wall to summon his manservant Gordon and blame the whole headache on him.

Gordon was annoying, as were all servants, but he had been the one who actually subdued Strat. Hulking and iron-muscled, Gordon had literally sat on Strat to prevent the young man from causing difficulties on the long route to Evergreen. Nevertheless, Walk would get rid of Gordon as soon as he had the Stratton money. There were just too many people around who had been involved in delicate procedures.

Delicate. How Walker Walkley liked that word. Last night, Devonny had been perfect in her delicacy. He had won there too.

Walk smiled to himself. Women must be shaped into what men required of them. Once the shape was complete, they could be discarded. He would buy a house to keep Devonny in, or perhaps confine her to the beach cottage, so that he could live in freedom and not be nagged by a wife.

"Mr. Walkley, sir," said Gordon.

The man was just too large. He took up too much space, towering like that; he made Walk feel small. "What are you wearing?" snapped Walk. "How dare you attend me in those clothes? What do you think you are doing, buying fish?"

"Miss Devonny had a visitor last night. I thought you would like to know. The visitor departed early this morning. I followed."

Walker Walkley paled. Could Gordon mean *a male visitor*?

"A beautiful woman," said the servant. "A Miss Lockwood."

❧

The wind over the Adirondack Mountains had risen. It carved channels into the lake snow. Like fluted quilt patterns, the surface glittered silver and gold and diamond.

Mario brought in yet another load of fresh laundry so that Moss could remake the stained bed. "Miss Harriett," he said gently, "how pretty you look today." He meant that the fever was back, rouge on her cheeks.

He had such a New York City accent. "How did you end up in the mountains?" Harriett asked.

"I was a Fresh Air Child."

"You were! How lovely. I always wanted to sponsor a child." Her guardian, Mr. Stratton senior, had forbidden it. Fresh Air children were certain to be unclean, and carry lice, and use foul language. Plus they probably stole from you.

The boy smiled at her. "Last year, fifteen thousand of us were sent to the country. The *Herald Tribune* does it. It's wonderful."

"And they let you stay in the mountains?"

Mario shook his head. "My parents died after I got

77

back to the city. I wrote Moss, who had had me for the week, and she said to get on the train and come up to work for her."

"Moss," said Harriett respectfully, "you work all week long nursing consumptives and yet you had time to sponsor a Fresh Air Child?"

"Children deserve a summer," said Moss. "Mario went fishing and wading and canoeing."

Children deserve a summer, thought Harriett, and young women deserve a life. Well, I cannot do anything about my life, because it's over, but I can see that children have a summer.

"Moss," she said, "send for an attorney. I must write a new will."

∽ CHAPTER 5 ∽

Moss penned a note.

Moss loved handwriting, especially her own. Hers was elegant and gracious, from years of penmanship in grammar school.

There were not many things you could count on in this wicked world, but the postal system was one. Her letter would arrive in New York City in two days. She loved the idea of news traveling so fast. If only it could be good news.

Moss never thought of the telephone.

There were occasions when a person might use that apparatus, but such an occasion had never arisen in Moss's situation.

Dear Mr. Walker,

Following your instructions to keep you informed of all that occurs, so that you may be of immediate

assistance in any regard, please be advised that inas-
much as she has decided to change her will, Miss
Harriett wishes an attorney to come. I hope you will
kindly arrange such a visit. I thank you for assisting
Miss Harriett in this endeavor. She is poorly. The
attorney needs to take the next train.

Your servant,
Kathleen O'Malley Moss

In the insane asylum, Katie was crocheting. It was one
of the few activities she was allowed, and she loved it.
From that slim silver hook and a ball of plain string
would flow circular lace, with arches and whorls, pine-
apples and crescents. Strat watched it pour off her
hook. In the background, the Melancholia wept and
begged and the Conspiracy muttered and gnashed.

Strat thought of Anna Sophia. Harriett had loaned
her a ballgown that wondrous night. He remembered
Miss Lockwood in lace, her hair piled in dark glory. He
remembered even the gloves she had worn, the thin-
nest, most fragile lace, the patterns pressed up against
his own palm. There had been nothing fragile about
Miss Lockwood except the borrowed clothing. He
wrenched his mind from Anna Sophia. "What happens
to the lace after you're done, Katie?" he asked.

She shrugged and went on crocheting.

"I mean, really," he protested.

"The laces are taken from me. I expect they are sold."

Katie's hair was thin and crinkly. Anna Sophia's hair had made Strat crazy. There was not the slightest curl to Annie's hair; it might have been ironed. Touching it was like threading silk ribbons through his fingers.

I'm thinking of her as if she is here, thought Strat. I'm thinking Annie, instead of Miss Lockwood, as if we are close again, and can touch again, and maybe even laugh again.

He focused on Katie's crochet hook. What uses might that slender tool have? Could he pick a lock with it?

Katie laughed. "You're going to get out of here eventually, Strat. I can feel it. Someday you'll see the hole in their strategy and you'll slip out and be gone." There was a tear on her cheek, which was unusual. Katie was so strong.

Strat felt strangely at peace with himself because he no longer noticed her misshapen body, just sweet Katie herself.

Then as usual, he *became* selfish: Okay, God, I'm a better person, so ease up and let me out of here.

God, as was usually the case, did not seem to be listening that carefully. So Strat talked in his heart to Annie, who always listened.

He remembered dancing with Annie. She had been so light on her feet. She and Strat had spun across the dance floor like autumn leaves falling from trees: at one with the melody and the wind. He remembered their few kisses. It was not decent to be forward with a lady, and all his gentlemanly self-control had been required, lest he go beyond the bounds of good behavior. He remembered best the kiss he had laid on her soft cheek, with which he had sealed his intent toward her.

I love you, she had said when she left him. *Be good to Harriett,* she had said when she left him.

The thought of Miss Lockwood and every other loss he had endured brought a single tear to Strat's face too, and then, to his fury, Dr. Wilmott was standing there, taking notes.

Patient weeps, the doctor entered in Strat's casebook. "You know, Mr. Stratton, normal young men do not cry. It is a serious indication of your delusions."

"If we were to talk about my delusions in your office, sir, we could solve them better than if we talk here, while I am strapped down."

For once Dr. Wilmott did not just smile and exit. From the safety of the door, he said sharply, "You are an insult to your family and to God. You attacked an innocent man trying to assist you. You will remain restrained. Be thankful that you are fed and housed."

❧

Walker Walkley thrashed around, half caught in the sheets and blankets. He scrubbed the stubble on his chin with his palm. He wet his lips. The name *Miss Lockwood* upset him badly. His eyes flew around his bedroom. All too well he remembered the ghastly sight of that girl materializing out of nothing.

"Don't just stand there! Tell me about her!" shouted Walk.

His servant said, "The cab took her to the docks. I

asked the maid who was sweeping off the steps when Miss Devonny's friend was leaving. She said Miss Lockwood was going to Albany."

Albany.

"She will have taken the overnight boat," said Walker Walkley. He felt excitement beginning to rise. What a chase it would be! And what a fine ending. *His* ending. The way he dictated things! That's how it would end. "The night boat is slow. People take it because it is spacious and elegant. It is a treat as well as a journey. I must reach Albany before the boat. Before that evil girl. So I will catch a train."

His manservant looked puzzled. No doubt the fellow did not know where Albany was. He certainly did not know what happened at Albany. Albany was where you changed transportation. From Albany you went north . . . to the Adirondacks . . . to Strat.

Mr. Walkley pointed to his wallet on the dresser. His man fetched it.

The wallet was empty.

So was the sock in the second drawer, and so was the silk-bound keepsake book where Walk kept cash between pages instead of theater tickets or autographs.

Miss Lockwood took my money, he thought. *How could she have known it was here? How could she . . .*

But Walk was one of the few who had seen Anna Sophia Lockwood come through Time. He had watched a ghost emerge in the road, and seen flesh come to her, seen her hair grow and her smile appear. He had seen the wicked clothing she had worn out of her own time—short little white pants and half a shirt.

He knew that she could do anything she chose. Now it appeared that she could scent out the locations of paper and silver money.

Walk sucked in his breath. "Call Miss Devonny's maid to me. Schmidt. Bring her here."

∽◊∾

"What was her name?" said Katie.

"Whose name?"

"The girl for whom you are here," said Katie. "I know all about Harriett and Devonny and Florinda, but I know nothing of *her*."

Strat shook his head. "I cannot talk about her. Not even to you." Then he was ashamed. Katie deserved the story. And what else did he have to give Katie? It was his turn. "Katie, if I tell you about her, you will also believe that I am crazy and deserve to be here."

"Start with her name," said Katie.

But it had not started with a name. First he had seen her: a ghost becoming flesh. Then he had walked a lonely beach with her, and laughed in the sun, and built a sand castle. "Anna Sophia Lockwood," said Strat, as if repeating sacred words. "She wanted me to call her Annie."

"Oooh," said Katie happily. "Let me guess. She was Roman Catholic and you agreed to convert and your father has you here instead of shooting you."

"No."

"You had a storehouse of gold, and you gave it to Anna Sophia's poodle."

Strat laughed. "No."

84

"I give up. I can't think of anything else involving a girl that would make your father put you here."

"She said she was from another century." Strat whispered in case Ralph was in earshot. "She believed she came through a hundred years of Time. She said they had orange juice every day, and didn't use horses, and could fly in machinery like birds, and not only used telephones but their telephones printed books for them."

Katie really laughed. "And they locked *you* up?"

He loved Katie then. He loved her for her good cheer and her good company. "Katie, I never told you that I'm sorry."

"Sorry for what?"

"For not getting between you and Ralph when you talked back. For letting Douglass be the one to save you, so they beat him too. For taking advantage of it so I could go outside. For running away to help myself instead of staying to help you."

Katie's smile was no longer hideous to his eyes, but warm and affectionate. "Douglass is full of love," she said quietly.

And what am I full of? wondered Strat.

For she had not accepted his apology.

❧

Steam was up!

Vapor rose thicker than clouds—more like blankets. Great gray swirls of cottony heat. Bells rang and people shouted and pipes clanked and water churned. At last, the steamboat pulled away from the dock and headed up the Hudson River. You would have thought they were departing for Paris, there was so much fanfare.

The Hudson River did not impress Annie. It was dirty-looking and it had dirty-looking ice on it too. The ice sort of hung around, as if there had been a party and it was left over. The steamboat paid no attention to it, but churned through the slush with an ugly whiffling sound, as if mashing innocent things in the water.

The day was grim and dark.

The steamboat was not romantic, but thick and ponderous and noisy. To her safety-conscious, next-century eyes, it looked ready to blow up. It smelled like mothballs and rotted flowers and sweat. People were jammed everywhere. The people terrified her. No woman wore makeup, and they uniformly seemed sallow and desperate.

Even the snowy banks of the Hudson River were pocked and gray. It was not a pretty snow. It hid no sins. It marked them out instead.

She was the object of considerable scrutiny from the men on board. The women were full of contempt for her too: she traveled alone. Of what worth was a woman without a man? Did no one wish to marry her? Did no father or brother care what happened to her? Could she not even find a clergyman or a cousin to escort her?

Her clothing was beautiful, and fashionable, and not the wear of a fallen woman. But alone? It was unthinkable.

The wind and the people were so cold.

The half-enclosed deck was like a vault where they

kept bodies until spring so they could bury them in the hard, hard ground.

"Miss!" said a sparkly bright uniform: red and gold, like a child's toy soldier in the midst of this gray nightmare. "You're on the wrong deck, miss. Come with me."

And the right deck, where the first-class cabins were, was as charming as an immense parlor. Individual scarlet upholstered chairs with matching ottomans were comfortably set around gleaming walnut tables, mostly occupied by stout men smoking cigars and sipping port. Port, said the attendant, was not suitable for ladies. What would she have? Coke, said Annie.

And when she tasted a familiar drink, how much less scary the world was, and how much less frightening her task.

Time changes go better with Coke, she told herself, and she grinned behind her heavy veil and her hat plumes.

❧

"Inform Miss Devonny," said Walker Walkley, "that she will have breakfast with me. Now."

Schmidt was solid and thick. Her heavy black dress and its heavier black apron turned her into furniture. Nothing to notice. Simply a servant. No employer ever thought of a servant as having a personality or a soul.

"Miss Devonny is indisposed," said Schmidt. She wondered when Mr. Walkley would discover that he was missing a great deal of cash. She wondered who would be blamed.

"Then fix trays. I shall have my coffee in her room with her."

Schmidt had not considered this reply. But she had a better one. "Female problems, Mr. Walkley," said Schmidt.

Walker Walkley nearly threw up. He could not believe Schmidt had said such a thing in his presence! Men should never have to consider the distasteful biology of women. He rallied. "Did Miss Devonny have an overnight visitor, Schmidt?"

"I cannot imagine what you are implying, sir," said Schmidt. "I am shocked. Miss Devonny's morals are above reproach."

"A Miss Lockwood," said Walker Walkley.

"I have heard that old Lockwood story," said Schmidt, "from the staff in the country. Before they were dismissed." She allowed herself a little smile at Mr. Walkley's expense. "The time traveler? The one who supposedly came out of thin air at the seaside? I cannot credit, sir, that you, too, believe in time travel."

Walker Walkley snorted. "She was rea—" He broke off, suddenly aware of the danger.

"Real, sir?" Schmidt finished the word for him. "You thought Miss Lockwood was real, sir? Did not young Mr. Stratton find himself in a lunatic asylum when he said that? Was this not your very own choice, sir, to lock up a man who believed in time travelers?"

The woman spoke excellent English. Hardly an accent. Really, there was no time in which immigrants were not infuriating. Either they spoke no English or too much. He said stiffly, "Will Miss Devonny be able to take the California train this afternoon as planned?"

"I shall inquire, sir."

"Get out," said Walker Walkley.

<hr>

"David," said Peggy Bartten, "let's set a date for the wedding."

The father of Tod and Annie Lockwood nearly crushed his popcorn box. "Peggy, we're just seeing a movie. We're not getting married."

"I want to be married," said Peggy Bartten.

"I've been married," he explained. "It's not what I want anymore."

"David, either we get married or it's over."

"Nonsense," said Mr. Lockwood, patting her knee. "Shh. The movie is starting." He munched popcorn. He loved the fake butter they poured over it. He didn't care whether it was healthy.

"David," she whispered, right during the first shoot-out on the screen, "I'm serious."

He patted her again. He was many things, and serious was not one of them. Women always dragged up this subject, and you had to make it clear where you stood.

<hr>

"Oh, Schmidt, you are brilliant!" said Devonny. "Female problems! I shall lean on your arm. Swathe me in extra layers. Since men never have the slightest idea what a female problem is, Walk won't be able to argue."

Schmidt hoped this would mean another tip. Devonny's tip at dawn had been a blessing. Schmidt earned so little, and had so many people to support. Paying for heat was difficult, and this winter was severe. Her mother was always cold. Schmidt's one goal was to keep her mother warm.

"Schmidt," said Devonny, "you will come to California with me. I need somebody to manage things. You are a wonderful manager." Devonny smiled happily at this decision.

"But miss!" said Schmidt, horrified. "You already have a maid attending you. And my family depends on me. I cannot—"

"Schmidt!" Devonny frowned. "I've made my decision. Now pack your belongings swiftly because Mr. Walkley will be calling for the carriage in a few hours." Devonny swept into her private sitting room, her silvery traveling gown whispering as it followed her around on the carpets.

Schmidt stood stunned. She had a brother who had never recovered from the war in which he'd fought, a sister who was tubercular, another sister who had been let go from her position, and a mother so arthritic and bent she could not get out of a chair by herself. Schmidt was the only one who could shop and run and go for them. The only one actually earning anything! How . . .

But Miss Devonny did not care how. It was not her problem. Therefore it was not a problem.

California, thought Schmidt.

So far away. She would be so completely, totally

gone. And yet if she did not obey, who would earn the money to keep her family?

California, she thought, dazed. She rushed up the servants' stair to her chilly cubicle and packed what she had: uniforms and heavy shoes and a coat not thick enough. But California is warm, she thought. The sun always shines.

Why, she was going to have an adventure—a great train—a vast journey. California!

She could not telephone her family to let them know. They had no telephone and did not know anybody who did. She would have to post a letter. Tomorrow, when she was in some other state, they would discover that they did not have her anymore.

I can't do that, thought Schmidt, her brief hot dream of California vanishing. If only I had money. If only . . .

But there was money. Schmidt knew of one more place where hard cold cash was kept. Cash Miss Devonny had not taken for Miss Lockwood. Cash that perhaps even Miss Devonny did not know about.

If I took it . . . thought Schmidt.

And money glowed as warm and sunny as California in her mind.

∾ CHAPTER 6 ∾

"Why, Schmidt," said Walker Walkley very softly.

She snapped toward the far wall. She didn't have a heart attack, but her knees folded. Her sight became blurry and her hands, full of somebody else's money, turned both sweaty and icy.

Walker Walkley smiled. "Schmidt, do you need money?" The man always smiled. There was something evil about the constancy of that smile. Nobody normal could have a smile endlessly tacked to the sides of his mouth.

Schmidt tried to stuff the money back. Wiped her hands on her skirt, as if she had not been stealing, he could not prove it, could not jail her, ruin her, destroy her and her family.

"No, no, no," said Walker Walkley. His smile never changed. "Take the money, Schmidt. I'm so glad to be able to assist you. Tell me, Schmidt. Do you have family in New York? Do you have people who will be cold, who might even die, if they don't have a warm place to live this winter? It's snowing out again, you know."

Schmidt could not speak.

"You keep the money," whispered Walker Walkley.

The whisper was more terrifying than speech. Schmidt was trembling now, her solid frame quivering like gelatin.

"Don't be afraid," said Walker Walkley. "Just tell me about Miss Lockwood. All the plans Miss Devonny made. Everything, Schmidt."

"Yes, sir," said Schmidt.

❧

"There will be only nine courses for dinner, miss," the porter said apologetically. "I will come for you when your table is seated."

Nine courses! Annie tried to imagine staying interested in food that long. She tipped him two dollars for squeezing the huge trunk, valise and hatbox into her stateroom.

His jaw opened so far that his huge mustache fell into his mouth. He studied the two single bills as if nobody had ever tipped him so much. In 1898, for all she knew, that was a week's pay. Had she made a major mistake, marking herself out as a woman who didn't even know how to count money? Or had she made a close friend?

The porter assured her that anything she wanted, anything at all, she was just to raise a finger and she would have it.

She summoned appropriate speech for a lady. "I shall ring if I require assistance." That sounded more 1898 than "Hey, great, okay." She shut the door on him and then let herself sag with the relief of being alone and safe.

How sturdy, and how lovely, the lock was. The polished brass was inscribed with the steamship's initials, a flaring ornate plaque with curlicued handles. Everything was sumptuous. The cab driver had certainly obeyed Devonny's instructions to do this first class. First class in America a hundred years later was not half so first class.

Dinner, therefore, was a shock.

Ladies traveling alone were segregated.

In a back corner of the two-hundred-foot salon was a table whose flowers were wilted and whose cloth was stained. The women who were unescorted by men were served last, and the food was cold. Nobody complained.

Annie's mother was ferocious in restaurants. If she didn't get good service, Mrs. Lockwood whipped her waiter verbally, explaining that she was paying serious money for this meal, and they'd better provide seriously good service along with seriously good food, got it? (People got it.)

The women around Annie were ashamed of themselves, and did not attempt conversation, because what value could any other single woman have? Most were in black; black was as fashionable now as it was for her mother, a hundred years later.

Annie tried to get comfortable, but her clothing was

not intended for relaxation. The corset Schmidt had pulled so tight was intended to keep Annie's spine vertical and her waist thin and her kidneys shoved up against her lungs. She had so much sleeve she could hardly manage her fork over the plate. Of course, that kept down the amount of food she could eat and made her waist even thinner.

"What a shame," said Annie brightly, "that the weather is so ugly. I would love to stand on deck and see New York State go by."

They looked at her expressionlessly.

"You'd be disappointed. There's nothing to see," said a woman wearing a ruby-red gown, a wine-red shawl and a rusty orange scarf. Perhaps she was unescorted because she was dangerously color-blind.

"Where are you all headed?" Annie asked.

The women busied themselves with their unappetizing plates.

"I'm going to a place called Evergreen," Annie added.

Their eyebrows rose in concert. A row of thin noses swiveled toward her, and a woman in black shifted her plates and glasses over, creating space, as if Annie carried a fatal illness. "And who," said the woman, "is in Evergreen? Surely no one related to you."

Annie had no cover story prepared.

Their pale faces, free of makeup and compassion, were like old cloth dolls. Their cheeks sagged and their hair was limp. They were nothing; nobody treated them as anything; and yet Annie was afraid of them. If she needed help, it would not come from people who knew what kind of patient went to Evergreen.

"My brother," she said nervously. That might work, she thought. I could pretend to be Devonny. Yes! I'm Miss Stratton, not Miss Lockwood. Surely I can wheedle my way in as Strat's dear sister.

"Your brother is in Evergreen, miss?" said Ruby-wine-orange.

This was good practice for whatever happened at Evergreen. "I love him deeply," she said. "My family has disowned him. He is in despair and disgrace. I, his sister, Devonny Stratton, am going to him anyway." She lowered her voice. With all the drama she could muster, she added, *"Without my father's permission.* For I love my brother. And he needs me."

How they softened. On their hard and hard-used faces was kindness, and Ruby-wine-orange said gently, "You will have to be strong, Miss Stratton. You are facing many difficulties. Will your family disown you, too, once they learn what you have done?"

Annie decided on the lowering of eyelashes to answer this question. Let sorrow be her speech.

It worked.

Ruby-wine-orange, introducing herself as Miss Rosette, took Annie's bare hand and squeezed it gently.

A band struck up.

Annie loved music. This music had lots of rhythm, lots of brass, and demanded that feet snap across hard floors. Her heels tapped and her waist swayed. And, indeed, it was a dance! Several couples got up. "Oooh," said Annie happily.

"You must not dance!" said Ruby-wine-orange, horrified. "There are *bachelors* here."

Harriett's doctor listened to what Moss had to say. "I am afraid," he told her, "that given Miss Ranleigh's condition, I do not think we should wait for the post."

Moss did not understand.

"You must use the telephone," said the doctor.

Moss could not do that. She did not know how. It was too much to ask. But the doctor turned away, for he had important things to do, and she, Moss, must attack this herself.

Stiffening her resolve, she went to the main building, where the billiard and smoking and guest rooms were. There, too, high on the wall, was the large wooden and metal apparatus. She wiped nervous hands on her apron.

Luckily the telephone company did most of the talking for her. Eventually the connection took place. Very mysterious it was, the way the voice came through the wire. She was getting used to electricity, although of course only for other people, not herself. She would stick with kerosene lamps, thank you, and not little glowing bulbs of bursting glass.

The gentleman was most interested that Miss Harriett wished to change her will. "I will come myself," he said, with such courtesy and understanding that it warmed Moss's heart. What fine people Miss Harriett came from!

"Thank you, Mr. Walkley, sir," said Moss, and she curtsied, never thinking that on the telephone they couldn't see you.

Walker Walkley's rage grew through his bones like a fever. So Harriett Ranleigh wanted to leave her money to a scrubwoman or an Adirondacker! The fool!

No doubt this Moss woman had infected Harriett's mind, not that it would take much. Women who received education were always at risk. Thinking damaged them.

Walk's brain was exploding. How could Devonny and Harriett—*girls!*—have accomplished anything?

He loathed Harriett. It would be no loss to the world when Harriett left it. Should he rush to Clear Pond? But if Harriett was in the process of dying, better Walk should let her die with the old will in place.

But what if Harriett called a local attorney and got this new will written anyway? Walk could probably overturn it; women were incompetent to decide these things. But it was messy, and he wished to avoid mess, just collect money.

And what about Miss Lockwood, on her way to Strat?

Walk must not do anything too quickly. Thank God he lived in an age of instant communication. A telephone call to the asylum was in order, but first he must think carefully through all possible problems.

There was danger here, and it must be other people who suffered, not Walker Walkley.

Walker Walkley ordered two carriages to bring the traveling party to the railroad station. He did not want to be in the same carriage with Devonny. He did not want to imagine her smug look, hidden by her layers of veiling. He did not want her to see his own smug look, since he knew all her plans.

The private Stratton rail car was hooked on the back of the California-bound train, and behind it, another private car—the Colts of Colt Guns—had been fastened. The Stratton car was trapped. But that did not mean Devonny was trapped.

Walker almost wanted to smash her between cars, never mind send her to California. But he had to have her as his wife. She would pay. He liked thinking about how Devonny would pay.

Walk tipped Stephens, the officer in charge of the car, explaining that Miss Devonny was upset about her brother and might actually try to get off the train and visit young Mr. Stratton on her own. Stephens was to be understanding, but he was not to permit it. Stephens, who loved Miss Devonny, and had loved Strat, was very sad and agreed that Miss Devonny could not be permitted to have lunacy touch her.

Walk could hardly conduct the conversation. He could not gather his composure enough to bid Devonny good-bye. She waved to him through the window, and he saluted her with his hat and was maintaining his bow as the train left Grand Central.

❧

Schmidt had been brought up in the Lutheran church, which was fond of guilt. Schmidt could feel guilty when she did not perfectly iron a sheet.

The guilt she felt over her betrayal of Miss Devonny

and Miss Lockwood was enough for Schmidt to hurl herself beneath the wheels of the train. And the money had not been Mr. Walkley's to give her, of course. It was young Strat's own money, tucked under his mattress, found by a maid months ago. The staff had discussed whether to send it to him, and decided that people who worked for asylums were probably thieves and would keep it for themselves, and it was better to tuck the money back for Mr. Strat, hoping there would be a healthy return.

So I've stolen young Mr. Strat's money, thought Schmidt, and I've betrayed Miss Devonny and betrayed Miss Lockwood and betrayed my entire upbringing and all my beliefs.

The train had a wonderful, almost soothing rhythm to it, its hundreds of wheels clattering over hundreds of track connections. There was a sort of safety in the repetition of wheel noise.

Miss Devonny was full of demands for this, that and the next thing. At least Schmidt did not have to go far to fulfill these demands. In fact, Schmidt did not have to go at all: the rail car had its own staff. Schmidt, to her astonishment and joy, had her own teeny little room. It was a sort of pocket in the wall, from which a bed folded down, and a sink poked out and a window looked upon the rushing world.

Never in her life had Schmidt had a room to herself.

She thought of the postal service, which whisked a letter in a single day to the proper address. She thought of the post box in Grand Central, beneath that fabulous dome of painted sky, where she had dropped the letter to her brother. A letter containing *one hundred dollars* telling him to spend it on heat and fuel and warm clothing.

Miss Devonny said, "What are your thoughts, Schmidt? You look so strange. Are you ill? Do you have motion sickness?"

"I'm thinking of California, Miss Devonny."

"California is a strange thought," agreed Miss Devonny, and then she required tea and hot sweet pastries and soft butter and also a map so she could see where they were heading.

Schmidt found the map, wondering if she herself were headed for Hell.

Since her porch had south, east, and west windows, Harriett had become a sunrise and sunset collector. She gathered colors in her heart: magenta and grape one evening, surpassed by sparkly gold or fluffy pink the next. Would there be color in Heaven? Would she hear the laughter of children there?

"Come now," said Moss robustly. "You will go into remission, Miss Harriett, I know it. A good patient gets another ten years, or even twenty. You will be one of those, because you are such a good obedient patient. An attorney is coming, but you must not think about wills and dying. Think about life and living!"

Charlie came to visit. A book of poems by John Greenleaf Whittier was lying open on Harriett's bed. "Harriett, you're not supposed to read," said Charlie. "It taxes you too much. Shall I read aloud to you?

Poems are best out loud anyway. And here's *Snow-Bound*. Nobody is more snowbound than we are."

But she did not want to hear Whittier. "You talk to me, Charlie."

"You would have loved last night's lecture," Charlie said. He held her hands gently between both of his and mourned that she was so cold, so limp.

"A naturalist from the Park Service talked. He was so proud, Harriett. It was quite touching. The Adirondacks are the largest park in America. A million acres. Just three years ago, 1895, the great State of New York voted to keep the land *forever wild*. Otherwise logging would destroy its beauty."

I will die where the world is forever wild, thought Harriett. I will be part of something that doesn't die. This world, when I die in 1898, will be the same world it was in 1398, and the same that it will be in 1998. "Keep talking, Charlie," she whispered. "It comforts me."

❧

Stephanie Rosette admired herself in the looking glass. She loved her outfit. She loved the hot intense look of the reds and oranges against each other. She loved how people cringed when they looked at her clothing.

Stephanie Rosette had lost her job in the shirt factory and was going to be a nurse in one of those huge cheap tuberculosis asylums. The kind with many cots in each ward. The kind where people go to die, not get well.

Stephanie Rosette was strong and tough, and she could nurse, and she supposed she would get used to the wilderness of the Adirondacks, not that she wanted to. Stephanie preferred civilization. Her last precious week in New York, she had spent the last of her pitiful savings. She had gone to the zoo and the aquarium, the symphony and the library with the lions in front and the Natural History Museum, saying good-bye to all the things she loved about New York. She window-shopped in the great stores: Tiffany's and Abraham & Straus.

Then she accepted her fate, and got on the steamship to go to a job that would last twelve hours a day, six days a week. Forever.

This short overnight voyage would be her final joy in life.

The beautiful girl who had shared the dinner table had been most interesting. Miss Stratton had slipped once and called herself Miss Lockwood. Most odd. A lady, definitely, but without a lady's manners. Sweet and courteous, but off-key.

She was startled by a knock on her door. "Yes?"

"Porter, ma'am. Miss Stratton, ma'am, wonders if you would be kind enough to assist her in her state-room."

Stephanie Rosette was puzzled but willing. Flipping the long ends of her orange scarf to help herself think, she followed the porter. She was big and bulky and her colors were loud and unforgiving. He was a little afraid of her, which Stephanie enjoyed.

Miss Stratton let her in quickly. "I'm so embarrassed," she said. "Please forgive me for asking you to do this."

One look at Miss Stratton's gown and Stephanie knew that the girl could not undress herself. She was buttoned and laced and strapped and tied. Stephanie shook her head. Ladies. Really, there were times when Stephanie was grateful not to be one. "You usually travel with a maid, don't you?" she said, trying not to be annoyed. "Here. I will get you into your night-clothes." Practiced fingers whipped down a row of forty tiny tight buttons in little silken loops. She unknotted the stays and released the corset. Stephanie unlocked the huge trunk and pawed through it to find night-clothes.

Oh, the beautiful stuff that lay so gently folded between lengths of tissue! Satins and laces, fur trims and velvets. Ruffles and pleats and eyelets and silk. The sheer loveliness of Miss Stratton's fashions brought tears to Stephanie's eyes. Just once in her life, how she would love a gown like one of these.

"Miss Stratton," breathed Stephanie, fingering the beautiful stuff. "How lovely you must look in these!" She thought ruefully that Miss Stratton's waist was about one third of her own. "Sleep tight. I will come to your room early in the morning to help you dress for the day. Do not open the door to anybody but me." Ladies had little sense. They believed the world was peopled by gentlemen, when in fact it was peopled by fools and rowdies.

There was something so forlorn and lost about this young girl. How old was she? Sixteen? And going on a quest that could not possibly succeed. She would only be terribly punished by her family. And yet Stephanie admired her. To save a beloved brother. Had not women since Antigone sacrificed for their brothers?

Sleep tight. No bad dreams, no lost blankets, no cold feet, no scary noises. If Miss Stratton's brother were trapped in an asylum for the insane, he had not once slept tight.

Stephanie prayed gently for the sleep of both.

Late in the evening, the same gentle attendant who had brought water and rags before brought Katie a piece of candy. A long stick. A peppermint-colored candy, whose sweet drippy scent filled the entire room. Strat actually forgot Anna Sophia at the sight of that candy. Six months of oatmeal, bread, baked beans, beets, and more baked beans had made Strat crave sweetness.

Katie gave it to Douglass. All of it. The entire stick. She could have broken it in five, and each of them, even Conspiracy and Melancholia, could have had a bite.

But Katie said everybody else had more than Douglass and that Douglass needed it most. Douglass was completely happy with his candy, as if he were not in an asylum, as if people really were kind and good things really did happen.

Strat thought about desserts. Fudge. Taffy. Chocolate. If somebody gave him a sweet, he'd gobble it down so fast he'd never even taste it, never mind share. How would Strat ever be nice enough to raise Katie's opinion of him?

He was thinking less. Using less of his mind. Around

him the weeping and swearing of Melancholia and Conspiracy seemed quite reasonable. He listened to it as if listening to a dance band. It occurred to Strat that the technique of Evergreen was working well: he was becoming less sane. As time went on, he would fit the diagnosis they had chosen for him.

He wanted to laugh, but his emotions seemed to have departed. He was just there, and Douglass had the candy.

※

Walker Walkley did not care for the Adirondacks.

He disliked uncivilized places.

He did not care about maple trees that turned red in the fall and spruces that went black in winter. He did not care about lakes and streams. He did not care about dead ducks or live ducks. He did not wish to wear red plaid, red flannel, or snowshoes. He did not wish to eat venison or trout, and he certainly did not want to snare it himself and get soiled and wet in the process.

The only place to be was New York City. Those upper regions of acreage should be called something else entirely, as it cast a pall over the great name of New York to include that pointless wilderness and those endless dull farms.

One might receive postcards from idiots who did go there, but one should not be forced to go oneself.

He had been forced. Devonny and Anna Sophia Lockwood had backed him into a corner.

Albany. And to think that the state capital was there, up where nobody lived or mattered.

Luckily Miss Lockwood had taken the boat. He, Walk, would take a night express train. It would be less comfortable. In fact, it would not be comfortable at all. It would be hideous and filled with the lower classes.

But it would be fast.

He would arrive in Albany before her.

And then there would be *two* patients in the lunatic asylum, put there by Walker Walkley.

He would see just how far through time or space the beautiful Miss Lockwood could travel once she was in a straitjacket.

～ CHAPTER 7 ～

How Stephanie enjoyed dressing Miss Stratton in the morning. She had put the thick straight hair up into an elaborate twist, and fastened it with a dozen long U-shaped pins. She chose a dress of deep green, layers of watered silk and velvet and taffeta. How Miss Stratton rustled when she moved! How her skirt filled the entire hallway. And for her coat, black, and also layered, with two capes, one short, one long. But no hood. Instead, from the hatbox, a delirious hat: a hat gone crazy with itself, a hat of velvet and ribbons and veiling and green wreathing plumes like ferns, and silk roses jauntily perched on one side.

Miss Stratton looked like a million dollars. And Miss Stratton had actually given Stephanie the mink coat. Its cut was so huge it actually fit Stephanie. Stephanie had protested, but not much. She wore the coat now, thrilled by its warmth.

The steamboat had arrived in Albany three hours behind schedule, slowed by the slushy river. It was remarkable that they had gotten upriver. Usually, ice closed off the Hudson. But although the winter had been the snowiest in memory, it had not been the coldest. At Albany, the water was still open.

Miss Stratton and Stephanie stood in a glassed-in parlor to watch the docking maneuvers. Railroads were not far, and all manner of horses and carriages and wagons awaited passengers and cargo. The activity was delightful: other people's labor was always so much more interesting than one's own.

How prettily the snow fell. Stephanie loved snow as long as she did not have to be out in it.

The dock was complete chaos. People were slipping on snow. Baggage was sliding on ice. The clanking of the great steam engines melded with shouts of porters and cries for taxis and yelling of drivers and swearing of teamsters. Hundreds of travelers were crossing narrow spaces cluttered with their hundreds of trunks and bags and boxes and cartons.

A few intrepid people had come to greet loved ones as they left the ship. A most handsome young gentleman in a thick fur coat and splendid hat strode back and forth, peering this way and that.

"Oh, no," said Miss Stratton. She stepped away from the window and put her hands up to block her face.

"What's wrong?" said Stephanie Rosette.

"That man on the dock."

"What about him?"

"He's— Oh, Miss Rosette, what shall I do? He would — I can't— He mustn't—"

Ladies, thought Stephanie Rosette. They are so helpless. She doesn't have a prayer of retrieving her brother. She can't even get down the gangplank.

"Will you help me?" whispered the girl. "Please. I am desperate. He is dangerous. We must run back to my stateroom before they take my trunk off the ship. You will take the trunk because I cannot be burdened with it. Yes, you are to have the trunk and everything in it. Will you lie for me? Please, Miss Rosette?"

Stephanie Rosette was actually rather fond of lying. It gave excitement to an otherwise dull life. "I," she said proudly, "am an accomplished liar."

Charlie kissed the pale cold cheek of the sleeping Harriett.

Moss said, "I want you to go back to your cottage in a wheelchair, sir."

Charlie shook his head. He was not going down that way. He would walk till death took him.

Snow had fallen again. In the Adirondacks, it often seemed to snow without thinking about it, the air full, as if snow just lived there, defying gravity.

Out on Clear Pond, where ice had been harvested all day long, snow covered the gaping hole in the ice. The hole had been marked out with sweet little treetops. It looked like rows of petite Christmas trees waiting for candles and ribbons and sparkling glass orbs. Neither

Harriett nor I, thought Charlie, will have another Christmas.

And Charlie hated Strat for letting Harriett slide toward her death without his love.

∽৶৶

Walk examined every departing passenger. He would know Miss Lockwood even if she dressed as a cabin boy, but she had no reason to be looking out for Walk. She would be the lady Devonny had dressed her to be.

A woman in a splendid mink coat approached him. Walk bowed, respecting the sum of money it had taken to acquire such a coat. "Madam," he said.

"Could you be Mr. Walkley, sir? A most strange thing has occurred on board, and if you are Mr. Walkley, I believe that none except you can handle this situation."

He was suspicious. "How do you know my name?"

"A young lady on board has had a fit of confusion. A most disturbing episode. Fortunately I was present."

"A fit of confusion?" repeated Walk. It had a ring of Miss Lockwood. Or rather, how people felt when they were around her.

"I really did *not* understand what happened," said the woman. "She is a *very* confused young girl, Mr. Walkley, and I consider it *most* fortunate that you are here to take *control*."

"What is the young lady's name?" breathed Walk.

The woman turned and walked back toward the ship. "We are not altogether sure. She gave us several choices. Stratton was one. Lockwood was another. It was necessary," she explained, "to lock the young lady in her cabin." She glanced briefly back at Walk, looking him up and down to be sure he was useful. "It will require strength to subdue her," she added.

Walk was smiling again. Gloating changed his face. His cheeks turned into heavy jowls. He followed the mink coat.

"I do not know what can have happened to the young lady's mind," said the woman severely. "I do hope, sir, that she will be kept confined in the future."

Walker Walkley was delighted to reassure the good woman that the young lady would be confined in the future.

❧

The instant Walk disappeared into the cabinway, Annie floated out. She might have only seconds of safety. "Just the valise and hatbox going with you, then, miss?" said Annie's porter.

"Please." The huge trunk required too much of her. Stephanie Rosette could sell the gowns or remake them. Annie could not be managing that vast container and the porters it required. Not in the middle of this nightmare. Walker Walkley! Here! Right upon her! It was too much.

The porter and carriage driver lifted her into a carriage without doors, designed to allow the huge fashions of ladies enough room, and her valise and hatbox were laid on the carriage floor by her feet. Annie wondered what was in them, and whether she needed it.

Off they went. The station, and the train north, were barely a street away.

She was stunning in her travel outfit: fabulous dress, sumptuous hat, veil, caped coat, boots, mitts, brooches. Nobody could miss her. Walker Walkley could so easily find her again. Yet Devonny had insisted that Annie needed to be dressed like this to impress the staff at the asylum.

It was a regular local passenger train. No private cars here, no staterooms, no sleeping cars, no dining car. Just transportation.

He will be only one train behind me, she thought. Please, Stephanie, hold him long enough that he doesn't make this one.

With the help of two conductors, she climbed the high steps into the gleaming, snow-trimmed passenger car.

It took Annie several minutes to adjust her yards of fabric: her skirts and capes and coats and bindings. She slithered on her own satin, but finally established herself in a seat meant for two. She took up all of it and could have used more.

With a cloud of steam-borne cinders, they were off for the mountains.

For some time, Annie simply sat, exhausted and safe.

When she tried to plan or think, her mind did not cooperate. Like the rhythmic wheels drumming on the tracks, her mind simply ran over and over the same fact.

Walk was upon her.

Walk recognized Devonny's clothing immediately. The beautiful gown strewn across the unmade bed was the same one Devonny had worn to the Vanderbilts' good-bye party. It enraged him that Devonny had given that to Miss Lockwood. He wanted to rip it up or strangle Miss Lockwood with it.

He was barely in the stateroom, however, when he registered the fact that no Miss Lockwood was within. No girl was bound to a bedstead, awaiting Walk's decision about her future.

He wasted precious seconds, thinking that Miss Lockwood had gotten out of her bonds by slipping through Time, hating her for having power that he did not. Nobody should have anything that Walker did not have more of.

The woman in mink was smiling. He recognized that smile as if it were his own in a mirror. It was danger. He tried to react, but he was too late.

Her scarf—a hideous, orange, unladylike color—was upon his face. He knew nothing except pressure and cloth and drugs.

Chloroform.

He tried not to breathe, but hungry lungs obey nobody, not even Walker Walkley, and he shuddered and went limp and then he was simply flesh on the floor.

It was good to be a nurse, and be equipped for such occasions.

A man who had accused that lovely girl's brother of being insane? A man who had kidnapped the helpless boy? Used lies and ruses so he could marry the beautiful thing and have her fortune to himself?

Such a man deserved a long-term delay.

Stephanie Rosette dusted her hands. She hung the DO NOT DISTURB sign on the outside of the cabin door. She followed her new trunk out onto the dock, summoned a carriage, and had the trunk placed within.

She hoped that the poor young lady's choices were wise ones. Most of all, she hoped that the young lady understood that she had hours of safety now—but not days.

And she, Stephanie Rosette, must make speed also. The man would be dangerous when he awoke.

Stephanie Rosette felt the wonderful sleek warmth of her new mink coat and thought of the money she could get when she sold the fabulous clothing in the vast trunk, and she prayed for the safety of a young lady who had no idea what she was about to face.

It seemed to Annie Lockwood that her train had gone so far north, she should be seeing reindeer.

Thick forests and logged forests.

Rocks piled in great slabs. Pencil-thin birches and the stunted tips of young spruce poking through the snow.

It was not beautiful so much as cruel.

Annie's heart and hopes seemed to have traveled to some cold and dread place also. She had no plans, only velocity. She was rushing forward as if she actually knew what she was doing.

Strat seemed like a myth. She was afraid of all that snow and ice. She was afraid of getting off the train. She was afraid of Walker Walkley behind her, and the asylum before her.

"Evergreen, miss," said the conductor.

The train stopped.

It was a genuine whistle-stop. The train stopped because somebody on board yanked the whistle.

The railroad station at Evergreen was a charming, tall cottage with scalloped shingles and a dragon's back roof. These were iced with snow, like a gingerbread castle.

Only Annie disembarked. The two conductors deposited her beneath a porch roof, set her valise and hatbox at the hem of her coat, accepted her tips, and the train left.

⮞⮜

"I don't care," said Peggy Bartten, actually stomping her foot. Mr. Lockwood had never really seen a person stomp a foot in fury. It was not attractive. "You file for divorce now, David."

"Peggy, the thing is, I don't want a divorce."

"Then what are you having this affair for?" she yelled.

He was perplexed. He was having it for fun, of course. Why must she get all serious about it?

This time she put her hands on her hips. "Then get out," she said. "It's over. I want a husband. If it's not going to be you, then I have to start looking elsewhere."

He tried to laugh. All of a sudden he realized that she was going to rip up the only clothing he had left: everything that his wife had missed. Quickly he stuffed his possessions into a suitcase. "What about tonight?" he said nervously. "We have tickets for that new play at—"

"Here's the play," said his gym-teacher girlfriend very seriously. "Either you file for divorce, or you're not on my team. Got it?"

He got it.

He went to his car with his suitcase and wondered what to do next. Vaguely he recalled his wife saying he ought to be staying with the children while she was away. Was that now or later? What sort of risk would he run stopping off at the house? Perhaps he would call Annie and Tod from a pay phone first, to make sure that his wife was gone.

"Yup," said his son, Tod.

"Yup what?" said Mr. Lockwood, feeling testy. What had given his children the right to get rude?

"Yup, Mom's gone."

Mr. Lockwood brightened. He had a place to stay. He didn't want to do this motel stuff: too lonely. Maybe he could get Tod or Annie to go to the play instead. The tickets had been expensive; he didn't want to waste them.

✄

Devonny stared out the train window. She had expected this to be an adventure and it wasn't. Instead of great cities, they passed through slums and warehouses. Instead of spacious farmland, recently logged stretches that were harsh stubs under dirty snow. Instead of pretty villages, worn and tired houses whose laundry had frozen on the line.

And she, too, was frozen on the line.

She seemed to have forgotten so many details. And what if she had not given Anna Sophia enough money? What if Miss Lockwood failed? Or lost her courage?

As the miles clicked by, Devonny realized that crossing the continent was the worst choice. She literally could never reach her brother now. She should have disobeyed Father and gone by herself to Evergreen. But Mother had done that. And they had not let a woman in.

"Oh, Schmidt," Devonny said sadly, "I'm worried about Miss Lockwood."

Schmidt burst into tears.

Her confession was short and terrible.

Devonny had truly forgotten something. She had forgotten what a skunk Walker Walkley was, and how his stink rested on anyone around him.

The train hurtled westward.

"At the next station," said Schmidt desperately, "I could get off and send a telegraph."

"To whom?" said Devonny. "I do not know where Miss Lockwood is. I have no way to warn her."

"We could notify the asylum," said Schmidt.

"They would just keep her from seeing my brother. Perhaps they would lock her up too. Certainly they would telegraph my father."

"Notify Miss Harriett?" asked Schmidt.

But a dying woman could not do anything.

And Devonny's friends in New York and Connecticut were also women and could do nothing without the permission of a father, brother or husband.

I don't want to travel through Time, thought Devonny. But oh! if I could travel through space! If only there were some way to fly off this train and fly to Evergreen and fly my brother away!

But time and miles were not on Devonny's side. Even if Stephens would let her off the train, she would be days behind.

"Schmidt," said Devonny, for the first time in her life using a handkerchief to wipe away the tears of a servant, "I do not hold you responsible. Walker Walkley makes people do terrible things."

Schmidt shook her head. "If I were a good person, I would have stood up to him, no matter how terrible he is."

They were nothing then but two women who had failed. "Because Walk is a man," said Devonny, "I agreed that he must be in charge of me. I must stop such behavior. From now on, I must say, I am a *woman*, therefore *I* am in charge."

It was too ridiculous. They both laughed out loud.

And the train continued west, and they continued to be women, and helpless.

❧

I am here just before machines, thought Annie. No chainsaws, no snowmobiles, no cars.

But there were lights. Not electric lights, but soft yellow gaslights in a strip of buildings across the snowy road. She walked to the hotel, grateful for its big painted sign.

How warm it was inside. How softly lit. She went to the desk to check in. She would have a hot dinner and a hot bath and think things through. She was perilously close to tears, and that must never happen.

"Yes, miss?" said a clerk most courteously. "Your booking?"

"I don't have a reservation. I would like a single room, please."

The clerk stared. "You are not expected by anyone?"

She started to shake her head, but this was difficult with the vast hat. A motionless profile was the only way to go while wearing a tower. "I am not," she said.

"You are traveling—alone?" said the clerk, enunciating his syllables as if to be sure of each and every one. He sported a thin waxed mustache. It really did curve in circles, like a cartoon of old-time barbers. "You cannot stay here, miss."

She stared at him. "You're full?"

"No." He pointed toward the door. She looked at the door for an explanation, saw none, felt very confused, and said once more, "I'd like a room for the night, please."

This time his finger stabbed more sharply, and Annie saw the sign.

WE DO NOT ACCEPT LOGGERS, JEWS
OR UNACCOMPANIED FEMALES.

"There are always rooms for people suited to our ideals," the clerk said grandly. "But doubtful or deficient characters need not ask." He sneered beneath his circular mustache.

When she did not move, he came out from behind his desk, lifting a flat section of the surface to pass through. There was a smile on his face, like the smile of Walker Walkley.

She backed away and he advanced on her, until she had backed out the door and was standing again in the snow.

The Adirondack Mountains blocked the sun. Blue shadows turned little Evergreen into a dark cavern. Huge spruce trees blackened the last of the sky.

It was like being in a terrible cathedral of night and snow and cold.

She was afraid.

And she was alone.

Only cruel winter was at her side.

❧ CHAPTER 8 ❧

By the clock over the railroad station, it was ten past four.

It was still the same day.

I won't cry, she said to herself. I won't stand out here in the snow and cry. If I don't get a room for the night, I won't worry about a room for the night. I'll go to the asylum now and see my brother, Strat.

She went inside the railroad station. It must still be the 1890s, because a clerk was on duty. In the 1990s the station would have been turned into a boutique open on alternate weekends.

The clerk in the station looked exactly like the clerk in the hotel. It was the beard-mustache thing, and the black-suit-with-vest-and-pocket-watch thing. She approached him.

"Where is the Asylum, may I ask?"

"Two miles north of town, miss." He stepped away

from her, finding things to do deep within his office, among his green-shaded lamps and tickets on rolls.

What would my mother do now? thought Annie.

Immediately she knew that both her mother and Devonny would make a triumphal entry. She had forgotten the towering plumes and the ermine muff. Instead of relishing the corset, which kept her upright, proud and snobbish, she was sagging onto it, as if it were a wall on which to lean.

Annie straightened. She sharpened her features. She tilted her nose, the better to look down it. "Summon a conveyance," she said to the clerk, as snippily as she knew how. "The day grows late," she said severely, "while you are fiddling about accomplishing nothing."

"Certainly, miss," said the station clerk. "I'm sorry, miss," and he hopped to it. In so tiny a village, the "conveyance" department was not far. A beautiful bell-ringing, horse-stomping sleigh crossed the street from the stable.

"That will never do!" said Annie imperiously. "An *open* sleigh? I am frail. I require a closed carriage. Kindly return that unsuitable conveyance at once."

I love this, thought Annie. Perhaps I shall become an actress, specializing in out-of-date stage plays.

The men tipped their hats to her, which she had read about, but never seen. They didn't actually move their hats, but touched their fingers to the rims, as if saluting. Annie was fond of this response, too, and thought that perhaps prior to becoming a famous actress, she would be an army officer, inspect recruits, and force them to salute her often.

"That," she said to the clerk, "is more reasonable." She tipped him two dollars, and he beamed and wished her a safe, warm journey.

The driver sat outside on a high bench, while she was within the carriage. It was not cozy. It was a small dark round refrigerator. The clerk brought a foot warmer: an odd little container of shiny metal, in which something hot rested. It felt wonderful beneath her frozen boots. It did nothing for the rest of her body.

There were so many advantages to the 1990s. Instant warmth alone was a perfectly good reason to move up a century.

The winter sun had not seemed to rise at all that day, and as afternoon turned toward evening, it did not seem to set. Gloom, the shape and color of crushed hopes, froze in the sky.

They turned away from the village, and passed through an evergreen forest that was not green but black. A forest in which children had rightly feared wolves. A forest in which wolves really did eat grandmothers.

Beyond the forest were meadows, wide and bleak.

The forest trimmed the meadows in an oddly circular fashion, as if cut by kindergartners learning curves. Trees rushed down to the meadow edge, and there, roots clutching rocks, the trees tilted dangerously, swept out over the snow like sails.

"Where are we?" said Annie through the little front opening.

"Evergreen Pond," said the driver. He flicked the

reins. "Bad accident here last week, miss," he said, gossiping over his shoulder like any taxi driver. "That's not a field, of course, but a lake, and it never froze up right. See, we had snowfall before the ice got solid, and then the snow turned into a blanket, see, kept the water from ever freezing. City people, here for a ski holiday, they didn't know any better. Rode their sleighs out on it."

He stopped talking.

"What happened?" said Annie.

He seemed surprised that she required more explanation. "They went through, miss."

"And were they saved?" she asked, horrified.

He was more surprised. "No, miss," he said. "The lake is deep, and the sleighs and the horses were heavy."

Annie gulped.

So the snow, which looked so pure and clean, had secrets too. Secrets the snow kept close to itself, the better to kill by.

Annie trembled, and threw the thoughts out of her mind.

The carriage stopped. Without the sleighbells ringing, without the horses pounding on the snow, she could hear again.

What she heard was a horrible chorus, as if some ghastly birds were gathering for migration. Croaking and screaming and wailing.

The driver hopped down and came around to open her carriage door. We're here? she thought. I don't want to do this. A lunatic asylum? I think I'm checking out. "What is that sound?" she whispered.

His face grew sympathetic. "Those are the lunatics. They scream all the time. That's why their asylum is so far out of town."

⤜⤏

Walker Walkley awoke to a vicious hangover. His head throbbed agonizingly. His mouth ached. Even his teeth ached, as if somebody had slugged him in the jaw.

"Somebody did," said the local doctor. "You had a real Mickey Finn there. Who doesn't like you?"

"I did not have a Mickey Finn," said Walk angrily. "Nobody slipped a narcotic into a drink. Some female held a scarf over my face and knocked me out with it. The same anesthetic dentists use. I believe it was chloroform."

The police laughed at this. "A man your size got knocked out by a woman and a scarf?"

Walker Walkley was surrounded by people laughing at him. He hated them. He hated all of northern New York. He would get that woman in mink, he would . . .

But the woman was nothing; she was a sideline. The important person was Miss Lockwood. He would kill her. No one humiliated Walker Walkley. Certainly not a female.

Rage percolated through him. It felt good. It felt hot and purposeful and certain.

He would kill her.

These pathetic little pretend detectives and this sad so-called doctor—that was what happened when you left the city; you got shabby excuses instead of competent people—would never find Miss Lockwood. Luckily, he knew where she had gone.

Evergreen.

He was many hours behind her.

But telephones, those blessed inventions of his time, were behind nothing.

All right, Annie Lockwood said to herself. I'm breaking into an insane asylum. Who should I use as a role model?

The driver offered his arm, lest she slip on the ice, and slowly, like a processional, they left the horses, passed between magnificent stone pillars, circled a snow-covered shrub garden, went up five broad and slippery steps, and approached the entrance to the Evergreen Asylum for the Deranged.

Deranged, thought Annie. De-ranged. Patients are cattle taken from their range: locked in stalls to be fed now and then.

I must not be afraid. In a moment, the driver will let go of me and I will have to do this on my own. *Who am I?*

Devonny? 1890s and proud?

Harriett? 1890s and brilliant and nervous and plain?

Florinda? 1890s and a flibberty-gibberty stepmother in need of constant assistance?

Or am I my mother? Tough as nails on the outside, ferocious in restaurants? Cut to pieces and floundering on the inside?

No! I'm Miss Bartten! I'm a woman who can get a man to do anything. I appeal to his superior strength, his manly personality, the pleasure of his wonderful company.

Annie added a sensual twist to her snobbish demeanor. She made her lips pouty. She filled her actress's mind with thoughts of adoration.

Whoever you are, you pathetic little superintendent of asylums, you are mine now.

Annie wore a veil over her face. It did not hide her features: its delicate black threads were woven in triangles, and yet it had the effect of sunglasses. She was truly behind it and others were distant on the far side of the lens. Or veil. It was *just* like sunglasses—sexy and dark.

Dr. Wilmott was tall, and the elongated suit made him taller, for the sleeves hung low, the jacket tails hung low, and heavy boot soles raised him up. His beard was ornate, carved around his ears, cheeks and chin. His mustache swooped, its waxed ends poking out into the air like Q-tips. He was very proud of this hair display, and continually stroked his tips and brushes.

Annie wasted no time. "Oh, Doctor," she said, for the nurse and the secretary to whom she had spoken both called him Doctor, reverently, as if he were God. "I am so relieved at your strong presence. I know how painful a reunion with my dear sick brother will be. I'm going to need your support." She thought beautiful thoughts. She tilted in a needy sort of way.

Doctor swiftly came from behind his huge, intimidating sprawl of a desk. The man actually knelt by her chair and took her hand. Annie allowed him to do this, but of course did not respond. That would have been forward. Plus, he was nauseating.

"Oh, Doctor," she said, admiring the disgusting waxwork of his facial hair, "please tell me about your achievements here. All through the terrifying journey on the train—oh, Doctor, that was so difficult—I have never traveled without my father before and I have learned such a lesson! I shall never take such risks again!—but all through that journey, I thought only of how you must be helping my brother."

Dr. Wilmott ushered her to a tiny hard sofa, so they could sit next to each other. She perched on the rim and kept her eyes lowered. How long would she have to simper over things Doctor had probably not done for Strat in order to be permitted to see Strat?

"We use the moral method, of course," said Doctor. He definitely never abbreviated his status. This was a man who every moment of his life and yours expected to be honored, because *he* was *Doctor*. "We treat many sad nervous systems, such as insanity, idiocy and epilepsy. Also, of course, cases of deformity."

Annie almost said, "What kind of jerk are you? How do you treat cases of deformity by telling them to have higher morals?" But instead she cried, "Oh, Doctor! I am sure that by your example alone, many have recovered."

Did he throw up?

Did he say, "Stop playing games with me, kid, and tell me why you're here?"

Did he say, "How would you know what kind of example I set, lady? You've known me five minutes."

No. He practically swooned.

She could tell just by the beard that Doctor liked himself better than anything else around. How much he must need to hear garbage like this. After all, he was stuck out here in the woods with a bunch of shrieking maniacs. Who was there to remind him of his superior brain and ability?

Only me, thought Annie. And luckily I have looks as well as brains and ability. I don't care what century you're in; beauty convinces people every time.

Slowly, as if in a ballet, Annie removed her veil. It was a surprisingly sexy act. She actually blushed as she revealed her face. Naturally she could not meet Doctor's eyes, but murmured, "Doctor, please reassure me that during this hour of trial, you will be with me, and help me face whatever condition my poor dear brother is in."

Doctor felt he could do this. He explained that the visit would have to be in his office. She must remember how severely deranged so many of his guests were. It would be too difficult for a lady of Miss Devonny Stratton's position to be assaulted by the sounds and sights of the other patients.

"Oh, thank you! You are so thoughtful. Doctor, you won't leave me alone with Strat, will you?" she said anxiously. "I shall be able to count on your presence, shan't I?" She had never said *shan't* out loud before. She wondered if she sounded as abnormal as his patients. "I have heard such frightening stories of guards in institutions like these. I won't have to lay eyes on such a creature, will I?" She fanned herself to show how appalling that would be.

Especially appalling once Walker Walkley found a next train. I'd better get this show on the road, she thought. Move it, Doc.

"I shall not leave your side" said Doctor, patting her arm too. He smiled reassuringly. A couple of decades of nicotine and little toothbrushing coated his teeth. Annie had to close her eyes, but luckily this was how ladies behaved.

Strat could not believe what was happening to him.

They were giving him a bath. *In hot water.* They were shaving him and combing his hair. *Gently.*

Strat was weak from so little activity, weak from the rage that had consumed him, and then eaten itself up, and left him sagging inside the restraints. His brain was flat, as if the asylum had ironed his ability to think. Maybe I am insane, he thought. Nothing is going through my head the way it ought to.

He could not help hoping they were also going to give him a real meal. Grown-up food, like roast beef and fried potatoes and gravy and . . .

Whatever happens next, I must not let myself think about gravy. I must think of escape.

He was too tired. He could not think of escape.

He could only hope that this lasted and lasted and lasted.

Soft warm socks. (They had not given him shoes.) Clean soft wool pants. (They had given him neither belt nor suspenders, so he was holding them up with one hand.)

He walked obediently between two escorts, too busy with texture and warmth and cleanliness to know much else. There was a change in scent as they went through a heavy set of bolted doors and turned down a different hall. No longer the stench of bad toilet closets and unwashed patients, but a smell both Christmasy and leathery. A sort of library-in-winter smell. He could sniff out cinnamon, too, and coffee.

And light!

A real window on one side of him with real glass, through which he could see a real world of snow-covered trees, and a statue, and a lamppost.

It overwhelmed him. Strat might have been a prisoner of war after months of suffering and isolation. He had little control.

In front of him were apparitions.

There was Dr. Wilmott who ran the asylum. Smiling and nodding, bowing and blushing. Yes. Blushing.

This could not be translated by a mind as dulled as Strat's.

There was a fine long walnut desk, a glass paperweight with dancing colors, and a lamp with a heavy brass bottom. There were books and the scent of books, chairs in dark green leather and a Persian carpet as fine as any back in Manhattan.

And a lady.

She wore a magnificent gown, as if about to leave for some gala affair. Jewels sparkled on her pale throat, and gloved hands were folded in her lap.

My mother? thought Strat dimly. His heart went crazy with hope. Harriett? Devonny? Had one of them come to rescue him?

She turned, and Strat saw her face.

Anna Sophia.

✎ CHAPTER 9 ✎

Annie had known that seeing Strat again would be wonderful, but she had not known it would be this wonderful.

She jumped up from the hard little sofa, caring nothing for the vast hat that required such perfect posture. She flung her arms around him. "Oh, Strat!" she cried, hugging and kissing. He was as handsome and fine as before. Thinner, paler—but perfect.

She had not one sisterly thought. All her thoughts were romantic. Plumes and ribbons and velvets were now halfway down her back. She wanted to feel every inch of him. She wanted to hold his cheeks in her two hands and kiss him for days.

She was out of breath with excitement. It had worked! Being a lady, being a flirt, being a liar—these things worked!

She wanted to dance like football players after a goal.

But Annie Lockwood had a goal of her own. Getting Strat out.

Strat, reasonably enough, was speechless. After all, depending on your viewpoint, he had not seen her in a hundred years.

Don't talk yet, she thought, let me handle this. "Oh, Doctor!" she cried. "You are so wonderful, Doctor. It is such a privilege to have met such a great man. What a cure you have wrought! How wonderful my brother looks! How deeply in your debt I am! Oh, kind Doctor! Your brilliance has no equal."

They really did talk like that in the 1890s. And Doctor responded as doctors did in Victorian times: he bowed in receipt of her praise.

Annie couldn't watch a man being so foolish. Anyway, she had somebody immensely better to look at. "Strat, darling," she said, "wake up, dear brother. It's your sister, Devonny."

"Devonny," he repeated. He nodded, as if tucking this away for future reference.

And now Annie Lockwood had a problem. She had Doctor where she wanted him and Strat where she wanted him. But Strat wore no shoes and no coat. His clothing was all too obviously the clothing of a well-cared-for patient, not a gentleman. The sleigh was waiting for her; the carriage was covered and would hide Strat. But it could not hide Strat from the driver, who might not cooperate with escape plans. The driver, after all, was afraid of lunatics.

She had not planned any further. She did not know how to get Strat and herself out. She did not know if

Strat was sufficiently with the program to pick up his feet and run. She did not know if Doctor had armed and dangerous backup. For all she knew, he had a buzzer beneath his desk to summon . . .

No, he doesn't! she thought. There were no utility poles leading out of Evergreen. And that lamp. It has no plug. It's kerosene. So there is neither phone nor electricity,. But it is winter out there, and Strat has neither coat nor shoes, no hotel will take us, and Walker Walkley must be on my heels. Now what? *Now what?*

"Doctor," she whispered. "Doctor, I am overcome with emotion. You must help me deal with this perilous situation."

❧

Only women got the vapors.

Even here in the asylum, no matter how badly Strat was treated, nobody ever accused him of hysteria. A man was superior to a woman. No man suffered from silliness. That was for females. Even Doctor had acknowledged that Strat was not hysterical, but possessed.

In the deepest recesses of his mind, Strat had worried that what possessed him might be something *womanly*. What if his father were *right*—there was no Anna Sophia Lockwood?

But here she was.

His Anna Sophia Lockwood. His century changer.

He was not just starved for food. Strat was starved for reassurance. When her arms encircled him, when

136

her soft cheek pressed his own, sanity returned to his body. His flaccid limbs, his tired brain, his fading eyes came to attention.

He swayed among dreams come true. Hesitantly, he touched her cheek, as she was touching his. Yes. She existed. Anna Sophia—his Annie—his Miss Lockwood —was actually here.

She was even lovelier than he had remembered. Her laughing bright eyes were real.

And the jewels that glittered in layers below her throat were Devonny's. She was calling herself Devonny. Saying that she was his sister. Strat had not one brotherly emotion. He wanted to dance with her— encircle her slender waist with his two hands and sweep her in joyful . . .

His mind stopped spinning. It was no longer a whirling wind of nonsense and failure. It was capable once more of thought. And possibly, also, capable of action.

What was her plan? How had she arrived? How was Devonny involved? What of his family? What should be done next? A hundred thoughts lined up in Strat's mind, and the first was sports: *I won*. Inning after inning, they beat me.

But I'm going to win now.

Weeping was over. He wanted to laugh and shout— and escape.

❧

"My dear," said Doctor, swiftly coming to the beauteous Miss Devonny's side, his hand reaching her waist.

137

He, too, was trembling. One of the loveliest young ladies he had ever seen was literally within his grasp. This must continue. She already worshiped him for what he had accomplished with her brother. Who knew how much more might be accomplished with her?

A fortune was within his reach. What sane man wanted to spend his career among the insane? Doctor wanted to spend his life spending. And nobody had more to spend than the Strattons.

If he had known there was a sister so brave, so loving, so beautiful, *so rich* . . .

The door opened.

His secretary said, "Telegraph boy, sir."

The boy (who was Doctor's age) saluted like a private to a general. "Telegram, sir. A Mr. Walker Walkley in Albany."

❧

Charlie, who had shot a thousand glass bottles into glass shatters at the river's edge, looked at Harriett as she slept on her deck chair, wrapped in her furs and woolens.

He had fallen in love with Harriett early on. But no gentleman could say such a thing to a lady who had a fiancé. Even if Hiram Stratton, Jr., had never written and never come, Charlie could say no word against the man, for Harriett loved him.

Charlie despised Strat for hurting Harriett. He could not understand a man who would abandon a lady. Charlie understood not coming to visit: consumption could leap from person to person. Refusal to visit the sick girl was sane.

But not to write?

Not to send tiny gifts from the heart—the book of poems, the box of candy—that made a hard day easier?

Every time he was with Harriett, Charlie yearned to speak his mind. Sentences lay in his heart like a stack of letters to be mailed.

I love you, Harriett.

I will take care of you, Harriett.

I will not desert you, Harriett. You are beautiful, Harriett. I love your mind and soul.

Harriett was dying.

Over and over again, Charlie wrestled with duty. Was it his duty to speak the truth? To tell this girl so desperately in need of love that she was loved? Or was it his duty to go on pretending that Strat, whom she adored, had an excuse for this?

What would God expect of Charlie? What would Harriett want?

From Harriett's porch, in the last spare light of day, Charlie shot bottle after bottle, all indigo-blue glass, broken pieces flying into the air, and thought how much he would like to do that to Hiram Stratton, Jr.

"I cannot believe," said Annie, in the hoity-toity-est voice she could manage, "that this secretary would interrupt so private and emotional an occasion!" Please let Doctor not recognize the name Walker Walkley.

Please let him not realize this telegram has anything to do with me.

She rested a gloved hand on Doctor's forearm. Her hair was falling out of its twists. Was she unladylike, or romantic and appealing?

The secretary said warningly, "Doctor, I believe it is essential to read this telegram now."

Doctor said, "Certainly not. Where is your sense of propriety? Leave the telegram, boy." He shut the door on them and apologized to Miss Stratton for the coarse behavior of his clerk.

"Oh, Doctor," she said, unable to believe how far she was going with this absurd language of theirs, "you were masterful."

He smiled. He believed her. Annie slid across the century for a moment, and wondered what kind of things Miss Bartten had been saying to her father that had been so delicious to believe.

※

"Where is your sister?" said Mr. Lockwood grumpily. The worst thing was laundry. You should not have to do your own laundry. Certainly Tod wasn't doing *his* laundry. It was a mountain in the hallway in front of the bathroom, since Tod liked to strip en route to the shower.

They were going to run out of clothing. It was a crisis. They needed a woman.

"I don't know where Annie is," said Tod.

"Well, you must know what friend she's staying with."

"I don't think I said that she's staying with a friend."

"Well, where is she?" demanded Tod's father.

"I don't know."

Mr. Lockwood disliked his son rather intensely at that moment. What made teenage boys so obstructive? At least Tod knew that men don't do laundry and he was just leaving it there.

"What did Annie say when you saw her last?" said Mr. Lockwood.

"She said not to worry."

Mr. Lockwood was going to have to wash a load of underwear. There was no other option. Furiously, he kicked the dirty clothing in piles, not wanting to touch anything with his hands. It wasn't his job. "When did Annie say that?"

"I don't remember," said Tod. "I haven't seen her in days." Tod, personally, did not mind wearing the same clothing day after day. He could outlast his father on the washing-machine problem.

❧

"Very efficient," said Annie.

"I knew this moment would come eventually," said Strat. He set the heavy brass lamp back on the polished desk.

Doctor lay messily on the floor.

"You didn't hurt him badly, did you?" she asked.

Strat truly did not care how badly Doctor was hurt, but on the other hand, a murder accusation would be even messier than Doctor on the floor.

"Oh, Miss Lockwood! I thought of you so often! I

141

could not discover whether I made you up or you really existed."

"I exist," she said softly. And then, in that rather fierce way he so well remembered, she gave him orders. "And don't call me Miss Lockwood. It's too formal. Whatever happens now, you and I are in it together."

Together, thought Strat. Is there a lovelier word? "Anna Sophia, you do not know how much I have needed somebody with whom to do things together."

Strat had touched Anna Sophia so gently, so carefully, during the other visits across Time. Now he hugged her fiercely. He needed to prove that his arms moved and he could still clasp, and tighten, and accomplish. He needed to prove that she really did exist, and could be felt and kissed and loved. No vapor, no dream, but a girl.

He kissed her in a manner he had not permitted himself the last time she visited his century, as it would have compromised her virtue. How wonderful were kisses that strong! With each touch of lips, she was more his.

A joyful thing happened. He found strength to pull away, and kiss no more. That was the definition of love: not touching a lady until marriage.

They took Doctor's pulse. He had one.

"Take his boots, Strat," said Annie. "His coat's hanging on that repulsive twisted wood thing in the corner. Wear the hat too. Add that scarf." She kissed his hair before the hat landed, and his throat before the scarf closed in, and they both laughed.

Strat undid Doctor's belt and yanked it out of the loops. A heavy ring of keys fell with a muffled clank onto the Persian carpet. Strat stared at them for a moment, thinking of the doors it had kept him behind. Before he threaded the belt to hold his own pants up, he slid the key ring on it.

"Good idea," said Annie. "Pretend to be a doctor yourself. That will please the sleigh driver."

"Why on earth would we want to please a driver?" he said, buttoning up the vast coat of Doctor's. It was far too big for him, which worried Annie. They must not look like escapees. But this was the Strat Annie remembered: somebody who did not notice servants. "We want the driver to take us away," she explained. "Very important part of the strategy."

Strat laughed.

She had always adored his laugh. She tossed him Doctor's gloves. "You'll be Doctor— Doctor— think of a great name, Strat."

"Dr. Lovesick," said Strat. "Dr. Timecross."

"Don't be a jerk. Dr. Lockwood. We won't forget that one. I know what we'll say. You're taking me for dinner in the village, where you will assuage my worries about my brother."

"Dinner is such a good idea," said Strat. "I haven't had a real dinner since they brought me here."

"I believe you," she said, pinching his ribs before she closed the last button on the huge beaver coat.

They dared not go out the door. Secretary would know he was no doctor. Secretary had read the telegram, which no doubt required a response. And no doubt the telegraph boy was standing right there in the reception room, waiting for Dr. Wilmott to emerge.

They went out the window. Here in Doctor's office, where sane people—people who gave him money—people who mattered—must sit, the windows must not be terrifying. No bars, no locks.

Strat lifted the sash. He went out first with his immense coat flapping and his beaver hat falling into the snow. He didn't look half so ridiculous as Annie, with her vast yardage to be squashed through, and her hat in her hands.

Dark had fallen. They need not worry about being seen. No exterior lights illuminated the grounds. After all, what visitor would come here in the night?

Deep snow soaked the hems of Annie's clothing and would give them away if anybody looked. But who would look, or could, in the dark? They hastened around the corner of the building. Strat's feet swam in the boots of Dr. Wilmott.

The driver was pacing back and forth, slapping his arms against his chest to keep his blood moving, stomping his feet to keep them from freezing. He had lit lamps on the four corners of the carriage, small yellow orbs which made the sleigh gay and cheery.

"The journey was so difficult!" Annie said to Strat. She handed the driver a five-dollar bill and prayed it was not so much that the driver would wonder, and think, and see the truth.

On the other hand, a girl who had just helped bop the asylum's superintendent over the head with a lamp and engineer the escape of a violent patient is not going to have a low profile whether she gives out pennies or gold bars. "Dr. Lockwood," she said, for the benefit of the driver, "I had to travel *alone*. It was so distressing. I am in such need of comfort. I cannot bear more travail."

Strat, being of his generation and not hers, took her literally. "My poor lady!" he cried. He meant it. "Alone! It is unthinkable. What a sacrifice."

"I love my brother," she said.

The driver was awed by the five-dollar bill. He earned seventy-five cents a day. With five dollars, he could buy two acres of land. "Where are we headed?" he said in the tone of voice that said Chicago would be fine.

Neither Strat nor Annie had made plans for this. Where *were* they headed? She could hardly say, "The farther the better. Just go."

She said, "We are famished, my dear man. Won't you recommend a fine dining place to us?"

"There ain't such a fine one in Evergreen, madam. But we could go to Saranac. It's not but four miles. A easy ride, what with snow. Smooth like. Take about a hour. First we head back to Evergreen, then west to Saranac."

"You are so clever, sir. Saranac it is."

She and Strat climbed in.

They had a wonderful time adjusting each other's clothing. The simple acts of pinning Annie's hair back up, of stationing her tower hat once more—these took half a hundred kisses to accomplish. And Strat's too-

145

big coat—it had to be unbuttoned, so that Annie could snuggle next to his warm body instead of the fur of beavers.

It was so romantic—a sleigh in the night! How the horses stamped on the crispy packed snow! How the silver bells rang! A slender moon and a thousand stars decorated the black sky, and the white snow smiled up from the cold, cold ground.

Before long the little windows of the carriage frosted up from the hot breath of two excited occupants.

"Oh, Strat!" said Annie, suddenly in tears. "It's been so long!"

He kissed each tear. That a girl would weep for joy at seeing him! It was too wonderful.

He held her against him, knowing that in this strange moment, he really did need, along with Annie, a sister, and a mother, and a friend. It was not so much romance for which he was desperate as comfort. For he was not changing Time, like Annie, but changing worlds. He was leaving Hell behind.

"Oh, Annie!" he said, his own thoughts too complex for him.

They wept together, and in some way Annie knew that she was weeping for herself, too, and her own damaged family, and she said, "Oh, Strat!" and then they giggled helplessly, because they had only a two-word vocabulary between them.

In the village of Evergreen, the driver paused for traffic. A train had just come in (from the opposite direction of Albany, Annie saw with great relief) and sleds were taking away baggage and crates.

The little train station was lit by lovely romantic gaslights, and some of the carriages had torches. A trainman carried a lantern which swung by his side.

The passengers were silhouettes cut from dark paper: trailing gowns, flowing capes, tall hats, pipes. Cuddled against Strat, Annie laughed with joy. This was what she had come for: the complete and total romance of the nineteenth century.

Harriett dreamed.

Once, years ago, they had all spent the summer at Walker Walkley's old hunting lodge, only a dozen miles as the crow flew from her cure cottage.

If it were summer, thought Harriett, if I were well . . . ladies in silks would rustle past, their ribbons fluttering, their laughter bubbling. Young bloods wearing corduroys and many-pocketed jackets would be returning with trophies of deer and woodcock. Fishermen would be flaunting their trout. Taxidermists would stop to collect these, and prepare them for walls. Stages laden with trunks and hampers and hatboxes, with folding tents and folding chairs and folding stools, and with rifle cases and cases of champagne, would be leaving the train station. Remember how we brought bales of china and huge rolled rugs, a dozen extra mattresses, chests of tea and coffee, and boxes of books and games?

Oh, Strat! Let me at least give you my last breath.

Annie and the boy she loved forgot the Time of watches and telegrams, the Time of telephones and police response.

They forgot the rage of a man who does not get his way. There is no rage equal to the rage of a man who has been made a fool of by a lady.

Walker Walkley would see her dead before he let her have Strat or Harriett or any of their money.

As for Dr. Wilmott, he was more sophisticated. He knew that Death is not the worst punishment. His own asylum would hurt her more.

And so from two ends of the Adirondacks came telegrams and telephone calls. From Walker Walkley and from Dr. Wilmott came promises to pay well.

And swiftly came men whose job it was to round up the dangerous and the insane.

The police.

CHAPTER 10

Through the coziness and the clinging, Annie and Strat heard shouts. Their sleigh began to slow down.

"Hey! Whoa there! Ho!" came bellowing voices.

The driver was pulling back the horses' reins. The horses could not simply halt because the sleigh, on a downhill, continued to move. But the pace slowed.

Strat and Annie let go of each other, bolts of fear instead of love coursing through them.

"Ethan!" A deep man's voice. "Your passenger escaped from the Asylum!"

A wildly excited tenor voice. "He's violent!"

"Tried to kill Dr. Wilmott!" A third voice.

There was an actual posse after them.

Strat jerked open the glass panel between the passengers and driver. "Keep going, Ethan. Please. We have money."

Annie handed him her final wad of bills and Strat tried to give it to the driver.

But there are some things money will not buy, and driving into the night with lunatics is one.

The sleigh reached the bottom of the slope, and stopped.

For a moment, Annie and Strat were paralyzed by horror. "We can't get through the forests without a sleigh," whispered Strat. "We would die of the cold in minutes."

"Then we have only one hope. We must stay a lady and a gentleman. Bluff our way out." Annie forced open the half-frozen side window.

The police were already there. "Has he taken you a hostage, ma'am?" they asked anxiously, and to Strat, "Do not hurt this lady. You are surrounded and cannot get away. Now step out of the carriage quietly so we are not forced to hurt you."

Annie prayed. No flirting this time. She must be cool and tough and strong. She must be her mother on Wall Street.

"Gentlemen, you have been duped," she said. "As always in my experience, a man who pretends to be a doctor is believed. I understand you think Wilmott is actually a doctor. However, he is not."

Strat squeezed her hand. In a calm sturdy voice, he said, "This lady is a representative of the Lunacy Law Reform and Anti-Kidnapping League."

"Is that so?" said one of the men. "Well, why don't you get out of the sleigh and talk it over with us."

They had no choice. Annie got out first. She held out

a gloved hand for assistance. She required them to help with her skirts. She wished for more light, so that they could see her face, but she would have to make do with her voice. "I certainly thank you for your prompt response," she said as warmly but as haughtily as she could put together. "It is so good to know the police are so quick. However, your information is incorrect."

"We've known Dr. Wilmott many years," said the policeman.

"And have you not dealt with our representatives during that time?" said Annie, arching her eyebrows even though this was invisible behind the slope of her hat. An actress must follow through on detail.

"Well, yes," said one of them reluctantly.

For heaven's sake! There really was an Anti-Kidnapping League. "Mr. Hiram Stratton, Jr., is possessed of a vast fortune," said Annie. "If you were notified by a cad named Walker Walkley, this is the fiend responsible for kidnapping Mr. Stratton."

From the way the police looked at each other, it was clear that Walker Walkley had indeed notified them.

They shifted a little on the snow.

Three police and a driver were ranged against a girl swamped by her own clothing and a boy weak from imprisonment.

Annie said, "We are bound for Saranac, where—"

"I think not, ma'am," said the policeman. "No matter what League you say you're from, Dr. Wilmott was hurt. We are taking you back to Evergreen."

Walker Walkley hardly thought of Strat or of Harriett.

He hardly even thought of the money.

His mind whirled at Anna Sophia Lockwood.

He paced at the station in Albany.

No train till dawn. That was what happened in the north woods. Godforsaken nightmare up here.

⤜⤛

Dr. Wilmott wanted to hit his secretary. How dare she posture and prance just because she had known the girl was a fake and he had not? It was necessary to hit somebody.

He chose Katie and Douglass.

It made him feel so much better.

And soon—yes, in this very cell—he would put the girl. Whoever she was. Who cared who she was? It was her suffering that mattered, and Dr. Wilmott knew how to make a person suffer.

He smiled, and Ralph the attendant smiled, and again he slapped Katie.

⤜⤛

Strat bowed slightly to the opposition. Annie could not think what he meant by it. Was it surrender? They must not give in! They must fight, somehow. They could not allow themselves to be taken back to Evergreen.

"Dear friend," Strat said to her, his voice formal, "allow me to help you back in the carriage where you will be warm."

She resisted, glaring at him from under her hat brim

152

and the rolled-up veil, which was now unrolling and making it harder to see and think and believe. "Trust me," he breathed. She did trust him. But those four were stronger. If there were a fight, he was going to need Annie. However, in a fight, she would be doomed by these ridiculous clothes. She couldn't even bend down to take off her own boot and hit somebody with the heel, because a woman in a tightly laced corset could not bend.

His hand on her elbow moved her toward the door of the carriage and Annie heard herself sob. She lifted the skirts she now hated, the miles of satin and velvet, and managed to find the first high step with the sole of her boot.

Strat shoved her hard with his hand, throwing her into the carriage like a suitcase. She felt the sleigh rock dangerously and heard Strat shout to the horses.

The men shouted, too, but one slipped in the snow, one was holding the reins of his own horses, one was on the wrong side of the carriage, and the driver Ethan was thrown to the snowbank by the force of Strat's driving shoulder.

They were off!

Annie grabbed the edges of the door and hauled herself into the carriage. Easier said than done in a Victorian gown. Seams ripped under her knees and the wind threw her hat by the side of the road. Oh, well, she had the hatbox here. She'd wear the other one.

Annie yanked the flapping side door closed, got on

her knees to yank the little front window open and shouted to Strat's backside, "Way to go, Strat!"

He was laughing.

Annie loved a guy who could laugh under these circumstances.

"I haven't forgotten how!" yelled Strat, turning the horses expertly. He was having a wonderful time. He was nothing but one more teenage boy, taking the corners as fast and hard as he could.

The wind through the open slot was sharp as a weapon.

Annie wrapped herself like a cocoon in the furs. In her day, furs were not politically correct. But what the furs really were, was really warm.

A sleigh race.

Horses in the night.

Moon and stars keeping watch.

Strat shouted and whipped and threw his body weight left and right to help at the curves.

Pines screened the moonlight, like black lace.

A fox barked.

And behind them, four men, presumably four angry and possibly hurt men, followed.

Strat took a corner too fast, too hard, and the sleigh overturned.

Strat leaped clear of the falling vehicle. The horses staggered, but did not get tangled in each other or in the complex tack. He was relieved by that—he could never have left the horses to break each other's legs. He would have had to clear them, and that would give their pursuers time to catch up.

He climbed onto the carriage side and opened the door awkwardly. Annie was shaken but unhurt. She could barely climb out in her skirts, but to take them off would mean freezing to death. She got out, and they slid to the ground.

Their pursuers' shouts and pounding horses were right above them.

"Into the woods," said Strat, and they ran, thigh deep in wet snow that clung and tugged and slowed and caught. Their feet stumbled on rocks and fallen branches at the bottom of the snow, and twice they fell together and crusty cruel snow tore at their faces.

Like crippled rabbits, they tried to hop over tangles and under branches. Tried to find a safe hole in which to crouch till danger flew by.

"Come back!" cried the tenor voice.

"You'll freeze to death in a hour!" shouted the bass.

"Don't go with the maniac, miss!" shouted Ethan, her driver. "The woods is terrible. There's bears and wolves. There's half-frozen ice and cliffs that break off from the weight of the snow! It's not a pretty way to die!"

They were deep among black and dreadful spruces, invisible to the road and to the four men and the huffing, stomping horses.

They had probably gone a hundred yards.

Nothing. No safety zone at all.

A horse stamped. Sleigh bells trembled softly.

They were all cold, and nobody had any source of

heat, but Annie and Strat were also wet, and wet was the greatest disaster.

The four men could simply return to their homes for a good night's sleep. When they returned at dawn, they would find the frozen corpses of Annie and Strat.

Devonny had told Annie to prove her worth. Well, she had failed. Annie did not know which pain was greater: the pain of failure or the pain of this terrible, vicious cold.

Nobody moved.

"Miss," said Ethan sadly, "the lunatic is not worth it."

But Strat was worth it. He had always been worth it. She loved him. Oh, Daddy! she thought, caught between centuries and sadnesses. Daddy, Mom is worth it too. Come back to her!

"Come back with us," cried the men. "Leave him there to die."

Strat wrapped the beaver coat tightly around Annie and pressed her to his body to give her warmth. It's my heart, she thought, my heart needs warmth.

"Does he have you prisoner, miss?" shouted Ethan.

Annie grit her teeth against the chattering of her jaws and after a long, long time, the two teams left. There were advantages to sleigh bells. Sound informed them what was happening. They knew, too, that both teams had gone back toward Evergreen.

"Come on," said Strat, "we have to use the road. These woods are too terrible to cut through."

"What if one of them is waiting for us?"

"One of them we could handle. We know at least two

are gone, since both teams left. And I cannot imagine that reasonable men would stand alone in the winter in the wilderness risking death. They'll come for us at dawn. But we won't be here."

They slogged back, falling and sliding. Her toes were so cold they hurt, her ankle was twisted and her face cut by the slapping of hemlock branches.

They reached the road. Moonlight gave it a faint glow. There was nothing in sight. They turned and ran toward Saranac. In twenty steps, they were out of strength. They walked. Tottered, Annie thought, would be a better word. "Too bad we don't have an all-terrain vehicle, or at least a Ski-Doo."

Strat looked at her nervously. It was this kind of vocabulary, vocabulary that didn't exist, that had caused some of the trouble in his famous essay.

"See," said Annie, "in my day it doesn't matter what the surface of the earth is. Roads don't count."

"Roads don't count?" repeated Strat. He could not comprehend her description of a snowmobile, for which barriers were nothing and to which no field or wood was closed.

They held each other up.

They could actually see the village of Saranac, a few lights in the night across a lake. Annie did not dare cross a lake after the story Ethan had told. What if they fell through where there was no ice, only a treacherous layer of snow?

But they would not live long enough to circle the lake. No human without the proper clothing could survive this. The police would come in the morning and scrape up the bodies like roadkill.

"We're not going to make it," she said. His lips were blue. Hers felt dead.

"Let me tell you about a friend of mine," said Strat. "Her name is Katie. If she can get up and keep going every day, so can we. We are going to make it. We're going to tell stories, and the rhythm of our words will match our feet, and we will make it to a building that is warm."

Annie tried to believe it.

"I'll start," he said. "We used to come hunting here, years ago, when life was good and my family was close. Autumn is the best season, of course. The sunlight is gold, the falling leaves are gold, and the hope that you will shoot a great buck is gold." He laughed at his poetry. "Tell me, Annie," he coaxed, making her participate, keeping her alive, "is it still forever wild?"

He meant a hundred years later. Had the stewards of this land, the people of New York, kept their bargain? She nearly said, "Strat, there is nothing wild left in my America. Only pockets of pretend wild." But this was storytelling, and he needed a story, and she said, "The wolves and the bears and forests of green are still there."

"Forever wild," said Strat happily.

"I, personally," said Annie, who thought that a nice Ford with a great heater would be a very good idea right now, "prefer forever civilized. Tell me about Katie."

He told her about Katie.

The story truly kept Annie going. "Why, Strat," she interrupted him, "it sounds like a cleft palate and harelip. That's nothing. Plastic surgery takes care of that when the baby's born. My brother Tod had that, and he hardly has a scar. He's handsome."

But Strat, of course, had never heard of plastic surgery, and it had never occurred to him or anyone else that they might simply sew up the deformity and be rid of it.

⁂

Walker Walkley wanted to rip the telephone out of the wall. "Where can they go?" he demanded. Every moment he had to stay in Albany made him more and more angry.

"Heaven or Hell," said the officer in Evergreen simply. "They won't be alive."

"You don't know that girl. I swear she has the devil on her side. Could they get to Saranac? Could they get anyplace else?"

"I couldn't. Three miles in that cold, wet clear through, and the cloth frozen to their skin? They're dead already, Mr. Walkley."

"Nevertheless, you warn those officials in Saranac, do you hear me?" Walk was shouting into the phone. He never quite trusted that wire. He said, "I can't believe you lost them to start with! Small towns! I would have thought you could manage a few weaklings like that without trouble."

"And did you manage the woman on the boat without any trouble?" said the small-town officer. "It was a woman, wasn't it, who—"

"Just you notify Saranac!" yelled Walk, slamming the phone down.

The Evergreen official put his phone down more gently. There was no need to notify anybody. Except the funeral parlor.

❧

They knocked on the door of the first farmhouse they came to. "Please," cried Annie as the door fell open. "Please help us."

Country people would not dream of failing to help. The frozen strangers were rushed in, their wet clothing stripped off without regard to modesty. They were put before a fire so hot it hurt. A stout, friendly woman in layers of skirts and aprons rubbed Annie's skin down, and put her bare feet in a basin of warm water. A thin, gnarled man with a gray spiky beard spooned hot soup into Strat's mouth. When Strat whispered that he would pay for a real meal—for beef and potatoes—the man grinned, and heated up a vast pot of stew: beef and turnips and squash and onions and gravy and potatoes. And Strat ate and ate and ate.

"Thank you," said Annie over and over again. "Thank you so much. Thank you so much."

"Whatever happened?" asked the woman. She was not suspicious. She was just comforting. Annie even had some stew. Normally Annie considered stew a sort of school-cafeteria idea: the kind of thing you steered

160

around rather than ate. But this was delicious. She, too, ate and ate and ate.

"We went for a romantic sleigh ride in the night," said Strat, "and I lost control. We tipped over and the horses ran on. It was entirely my fault. If I had killed us both by us freezing in the night, I would have none to blame but myself."

"Well, now," said the woman comfortably, "didn't happen, did it? Now, we got no extra beds, but you'll curl up on the rug by the stove and be warm for the night. Whoever's worrying about you, they'll just have to worry till morning."

And they were wrapped in rugs, and left to sleep the night in peace. Annie was asleep in a moment, but Strat required no sleep. He had had a lot of sleeping in the last year.

He stared at Annie, asleep in the firelight.

How undefended she was in her sleep.

How young.

She had saved him, and in return he had nearly gotten her killed. It was so difficult to believe in himself as a person of worth. But Anna Sophia believed in him. She had crossed a century to come to him.

In the shadows, his hand a dark quiver by the light of the fading fire, he touched a strand of her hair. It was hot from lying near the embers. He wove it between his fingers, and thought of love, and Annie, and Harriett, and Katie. And he—supposedly a gentleman—what was he to do now? There must be a wise course to follow. But what was it?

By dawn's early light, police from both Saranac and

Evergreen would converge on the place where they had abandoned the sleigh. If they bothered to call the Anti-Kidnapping League on Fourteenth Street, they would know that Annie had not been employed by them. She was no innocent to be rescued from the maniac. Annie was in as much trouble as he was. Much as Doctor deserved death, Strat hoped that he had survived—if Strat and Annie had killed the man, hordes of police would descend upon them.

Strat and Annie must be gone and leave no tracks. How? In such snow, with so many witnesses? What must they do, and in what order? Where could they flee to?

At four in the morning, Strat got up and dressed. Annie's clothing was dry now, draped on a wooden clotheshorse by the kitchen coal stove. She slept in a ball, a mass of long dark hair hanging out of the furs and spread across the braided rug. He touched her hot cheek.

She woke instantly, throwing off the fur like a stranger.

She was wearing a huge white nightdress their hostess had brought. It buttoned right up to the throat, had long sleeves that tightly clasped her wrists, and reached to her toes.

Strat averted his eyes. It was a trespass, that he should see her in her nightclothes.

Annie herself woke up fast. She remembered all of it instantly: their whole success and their whole failure.

When Strat turned from the sight of her in her

nightie, she grinned. I love these 1890s guys. They're so cute. Well, one of them anyway.

She tucked herself up against him, snuggling until she found a really good hug spot, and they whispered. Travel could not occur until daylight and Strat was bursting with need. He told Annie about Walk and the essay and his professor and the accusations and his own father's betrayal.

Annie kissed his hand. Even his fingers were thin. "Oh, Strat! They were so terrible to you."

"Nobody ever even wrote to me!" Strat cried out, his whisper emotional and hurt. "Nobody ever came. Not my mother, not my sister, not even Harriett, who I thought would come to me over hell or high water."

"Your mother came," Annie told him. "She sold jewels to buy her ticket. Dr. Wilmott wouldn't let her in. He said it would disturb your treatment. As for Devonny, your sister wrote you all the time. But she has been almost a prisoner of Walker Walkley, and Walk interfered with the mail. None of Devonny's letters ever left the house."

"Walk handled the mail? But where are Father and Florinda?"

"Florinda and your father went out to California several months ago. Your father has decided there is more money to be made on the West Coast than on the East."

"How ridiculous," said Strat. "There's nothing out there but orange trees."

"Trust me, Strat, he's right on this one," said Annie. "Anyway, your father pretty much left everything in

Walker Walkley's hands. And you know those are sick and greedy hands."

"And Harriett?" he whispered. He knew how hard this question would be, for both Annie and Harriett had loved him: loved him at the same time, with the same hope.

How Annie wanted to skip the topic of Harriett. Strat's fiancée. In his own Time, Strat was a gentleman. In her Time, Annie was not acquainted with many boys to whom manners mattered. But being a gentleman also involved honor. And Strat, a man of honor, would want to do the right thing by the ladies in his world. She, Annie, must also do the right thing by the people in this life.

Annie set out the facts harshly and fast. "Harriett has consumption. She is at a cure cottage at Clear Pond, recovering her strength. Devonny instructed me to take you to her if at all possible. Harriett doesn't know you were locked in Evergreen. She was already at Clear Pond. In fact, I'm guessing that Walker Walkley coordinated things so neither of you would know the truth about the other. Your father and Walker Walkley felt that being told about your insanity would be another burden for her bad health. They said she could not bear the news that you had become insane."

Strat sat, as far removed from Annie as Time, caught in the world he had had once and did not have now. "Anna Sophia, I have some very ugly people in my life."

Truly, thought Annie. I'm luckier. Nobody in my life is so ugly. Not even Miss Bartten, or Dad. They're peo-

164

ple who want everything their own way, even if it hurts the rest of us. But they aren't vicious.

Or are they? What would Mom say?

"Annie," said Strat finally, close enough to her in his heart to use the precious nickname, "does my poor Harriett think I have abandoned her?"

"I don't know. Devonny didn't know. I bet Walk stole Harriett's letters to Devonny too."

"We will go to Harriett then," said Strat. He was relieved, actually. It gave them a destination, and a very important one. He wasn't running away if he went to Harriett. He was her knight, her soldier, her fiancé.

"But Strat," protested Annie, "Walk will guess that that's where you'd go. Won't the police just follow us? Or be waiting for us? I think we should head for some city where we can vanish, and go see Harriett later."

For a few moments, he simply held on to her, fingering her silky hair, wondering what it could be like to live in a Time where disease was conquered. "There might not be a later for Harriett," he said tiredly. *Oh Dear God*, he prayed, for suddenly God was dear, and so was life, and so were Harriett and Annie; *Dear God, let me reach Harriett in time.*

The mantel clock chimed five.

Annie felt ambushed by Time and by facts. *I am taking the man I love to the woman who loves him*, she realized. *They are engaged. People do not take that lightly whatever century they occupy. I don't want Harriett to have Strat now. Not after all this.*

But what would I do with Strat after I have him?

Take him home with me to my century, like a prize at the bottom of the cereal box? Or would I stay with him in his century? Flee to Canada or California?

Strat, I love you so! But where is the right way for us? There must be one, or Time would not have brought me here. But what is it? How can both Harriett and I have you?

"Get dressed," instructed Strat. "These people probably have a cutter and a horse. We'll leave money, as much as we can, so they cannot accuse us of stealing. Write a note. Explain that we cannot wait for them to get up."

Annie was still doubtful. "I think it would be better if—"

Strat kissed her. It was not affection. It was a kiss to close her lips. "I know best, Anna Sophia. Don't worry your little head anymore. You have done very well to get so far, and I'll handle it from now on."

She had the brief thought that being a gentleman in Strat's Time was also being a very pushy chauvinist, but she set the thought aside, as many a woman had done, and let him handle it as he saw fit.

◈

Annie's dress had dried in a million wrinkles. It was torn in several places and stained everywhere. The coat had survived no better. One of the two capes was hanging from threads, so she ripped it away, and then the coat looked positively deformed. She appropriated Doctor's plaid scarf, tying it around her head to protect her ears. Immediately she ceased to be a lady of wealth and station, and became an immigrant in pitiful hand-me-downs.

I'll whip Strat into shape, she decided. He believes men are destined to be in charge and ladies exist to say Yes and Thank You. I'm glad so much has changed in a hundred years.

In thinking of her own mother, however, Annie was hard-pressed to be sure that anything had changed.

At any rate, when she went outdoors, not only was the cutter ready and the horse harnessed but Strat was paying the husband, and this arrangement seemed to be just fine with everybody, and even reasonable.

The man kindly gave them road directions for Clear Pond, including a way to bypass Saranac Village, and they were off, minutes before first light. The cutter skimmed over packed snow. The dawning sun exploded. A fireball of crimson. The sky matched the finest jewels from Tiffany's.

In a few hours, they came to a village, where shops had begun to open. "We must bring Harriett a present," Strat insisted, so they stopped at stores and finally settled on a candy box: fifty sticks in colors and flavors Annie hardly knew: black paregoric, yellow molasses, brown horehound, birch, sassafras, and vanilla cream.

They had luncheon at an inn by the side of a lake which had been plowed clear of snow. Big clumsy iceboats and skaters in bright red were slipping and sliding everywhere. Children were laughing, and bonfires on the shore were surrounded by people warming their hands. Sellers of hot chocolate were making the rounds. Annie loved the little kids' skates: funny little two-knifed shoes. These kids stared in envy at the few who wore white lace-up boot skates. A few men were skating actually *backward*, and everybody was awe-struck.

They were not at Olympic levels here. But they were happy.

Strat and Annie sat in a wonderful dining room—huge peeled logs wrapping an immense two-story field-stone fireplace in which a fire as tall as Annie burned. They held hands and talked and watched the laughing children come and go.

"I'm so glad to see happy, normal people," said Strat. "It's been so long for me—happiness or normalcy."

Happiness or normalcy, thought Annie Lockwood, with a little shiver. Shouldn't they go together? Shouldn't it be happiness *and* normalcy? Are we going to have to choose one or the other?

And Harriett—is she the one who will make Strat happy? Or am I?

And what do I want?

⁂ CHAPTER 11 ⁂

The sun turned the snow to ribbons of gold, and the shadows of balsam and birch belonged on Christmas cards. The sky was shot with glitter and the frozen waterfalls were museum pieces.

Clear Pond was quite literally around the next bend. It was the most beautiful mile of all the beautiful miles they had come. It had its own entry lane: a swooping white road cut into white snow walls. It had its own lake, of course, an unplowed expanse of snow with funny little tiny trees peeking out here and there, way out in the middle of the pond. The sanitarium buildings were constructed from rough-hewn vertical logs trimmed in wooden lace.

It was exceptionally quiet, as if a president had died. All over the grounds, young men were leaning on their male nurses and having cigarettes or cigars or pipes.

"They're dying of lung disease and they still *smoke*?" said Annie.

Strat looked startled, as if there were no connection between smoke and lungs.

Annie and Strat found the main building and entered the office, where they were greeted by a woman dressed far better than Annie was.

"I am Hiram Stratton, Jr.," said Strat. "I am engaged to Miss Harriett Ranleigh."

The woman turned hard and disapproving. "And I," she said, "am Mrs. Havers. Miss Harriett has written you over and over, Mr. Stratton, begging for your presence. You come now, when she is in the arms of death?"

Arms of death? How horrible! thought Annie. Does Death have arms? A long reach and thin fingers and sharp nails?

"No," said Strat, too softly, as if his heart were lying with that syllable. It wasn't really *No*. It was *Yes, but I hoped I was wrong*. "She can't be. I can't have come too late."

He loves her! thought Annie, and her heart, too, lay crushed within that syllable.

"You have. What is your excuse for such vile behavior?" asked Mrs. Havers flatly.

If only we accused each other of vile behavior in my day, thought Annie. We're too busy being politically correct to admit that some people are just vile. And Strat knows so many of them.

"I have been imprisoned," said Strat, "in an asylum. Relatives wanted my money. They created lies about me and kidnapped me. No letter I wrote Harriett was ever mailed."

He had forgotten Anna Sophia. He was entreating Mrs. Havers as if she were an angel of judgment. "I beg you to believe me." He had never looked more appealing. His shaggy hair fell forward. His formal clothing hung around him with a sort of strength, as if he would fill it any moment. "I am perfectly safe, madam," he said. "I love Harriett. I must be with her."

The woman softened. "Yes," she said. "You must." For a moment, they were both angels: people doing their very best in a terrible situation.

Then, briskly, Mrs. Havers surveyed Annie and the wrinkled badly matched outfit. "Good. Another servant. Your name?"

Annie was so startled she told the truth. "Annie Lockwood." I don't think I want to be a servant, she thought. She expected Strat to deny this unwanted status. But he didn't. As they left the office, Mrs. Havers said over her shoulder, "Lockwood! Carry those bags."

What was with these people? On the one hand, they didn't want you to lift an ungloved finger. On the other hand, if you were a servant, you'd better lift, and lift fast. No backtalk. Annie struggled to hoist a large assembly of cartons without hurting her back.

"Lockwood! Don't dillydally."

Annie grunted.

"She has no manners," said the woman to Strat.

Strat apologized for Annie's failure to say "Yes, ma'am."

Being a lady was tons of fun, plus you got great hats.

Being a servant had already worn thin. Annie wasn't going to last long as a combination nurse and grocery cart. She wasn't ready to say "Yes ma'am." She was ready to tell Strat where to go, and how much to carry while he went there.

❧

Walker Walkley could not believe how swiftly the tide had turned. The so-called police in Evergreen had found no frozen corpses. The so-called police in Saranac had found no trace of Strat and Miss Lockwood.

The only possibility now was Clear Pond, and Harriett Ranleigh. Miss Lockwood had retrieved Strat like a duck from a pond, and even now Strat was probably controlling Harriett. What if Harriett were swept to health by the mere presence of Strat? Where would her money go then? To Strat! Not Walk!

Devonny had engineered this. A vixen with no intention of marrying Walk, just a lying conniving female.

I will have that money, Walk thought over and over. The money glistened in his mind. It was the color of the ice under the sun. The color of silver and gold.

But at last, in Evergreen of all unlikely places, he had an ally.

Dr. Wilmott said, "I beg of you, Mr. Walkley. Permit me to go with you to Clear Pond. I, too, have scores to settle, and an inmate to return to his cell."

"Perhaps, Wilmott," said Walk, who considered doctors merely educated servants, "you will have room for another inmate."

"I am sure we could accommodate Miss Lockwood,"

said Dr. Wilmott. "Of course, there is the matter of payment."

"Bill me," said Walker Walkley.

❧

Annie was shocked.

No gentle pallor, no rosy cheeks, no sweet fading girl.

How could this be Harriett? The Harriett of Annie's other trip through Time had danced and played croquet and raced upstairs and strolled on the beach.

Harriett's face was hollow and gaunt. Her limbs had become sticks from which muscles had melted off, leaving only skin. Each joint was a knot on a twig. Her fingers were bone, covered with white parchment. Harriett was gasping, her lungs too compromised to fill. The room was harsh with the sucking struggle for air.

So this was why they called it consumption. It had eaten Harriett.

Harriett stared at the man before her, throwing his greatcoat and hat and gloves to the invisible servant—Annie. "Strat," Harriett breathed. "Oh, Strat. Oh, thank you. Oh, dear sweet God, thank you." Harriett was addressing them both at once: God and Strat. She had no more voice than she had flesh: there was only a whisper of her left to the world.

Strat sat on the edge of her bed and wrapped her and her blankets in his arms. Rocking her back and forth, he murmured, "Harriett, Harriett. I cannot believe this happened to either of us. Harriett, I loved you all along.

173

I truly did." He kissed her lips, which no healthy person must ever do with a consumptive.

But Annie was glad. Yes, this was right. It would be like Sleeping Beauty. Strat was Prince Charming. He would kiss away death and sorrow.

She loved it: a fairy-tale ending, and everybody living happily ever after.

Except me, she thought. What am I supposed to do?

Strat kissed Harriett's thin, dry hair and the hands so weak they could not press back against his. Gently and briefly, he told her what had happened to him, the dreadful reasons he had not been at her side before.

"Oh, Strat," said Harriett, her thready voice thicker from relief. "You have been suffering too. I didn't know. I thought you had found another to love."

I'm the other, thought Annie. Harriett thought that I . . . *and I would have.* I love Strat. I want to be his other. But there is no way to divide a man. No matter which century.

Annie pressed against the wall. Harriett had not thought to glance at her. In this clothing, she was merely a person to change the linen, fill the hot water bottle, and stoke the stove.

"You will get well now, darling Harriett," said Strat.

In every motion of their embrace was their history together: for Strat and Harriett had known each other from childhood, and when she was orphaned, Harriett had become Mr. Stratton's ward, and Harriett and Devonny had been best friends, and it had always been expected that Strat and Harriett would wed.

Only the appearance of Anna Sophia Lockwood in 1895 had interrupted the flow of events.

But I've put it back together, thought Annie. All the king's horses and all the king's men—who needs them? Just call me.

"I will take you away, Harriett," said Strat. "I know doctors approve of ice-cold air for the lungs, but I have been cold this winter and I have come to believe in warmth. I will take you to Mexico. Think of heat, Harriett, and golden sun. Think of love, and our children, and the home we will make for them."

Annie's soul leaped a hundred years. Was Daddy saying this to Miss Bartten? Were they planning a vacation in Mexico, thinking up baby names for a new family? But what about *our* family? cried Annie. The people who come first should stay first!

"I have thought of nothing else for so long," said Harriett. She found the strength to touch his cheek. In her terrible wasted condition, she became somehow beautiful: love did transform her.

And it was not her own love, because she had loved Strat all along; it was Strat's love, confirming that Harriett mattered, that he adored her.

"Would you leave us?" said Strat to the nurse and to Annie. The nurse, whose nametag said MOSS, took Annie's arm and led her out of the sickroom. Annie did not mind. She hurt all over, for love was too complex and went in too many directions and involved too many people.

I want true love to save Harriett, she thought.

But I want true love for myself.

Strat's true love.

In the asylum at Evergreen, Katie did not cry. The loss of Strat was too great and awful for mere tears. Strat's company had held her together against the assault of the asylum.

God forgive me this sin, she thought. Strat has escaped and instead of rejoicing for him, I want him caught and brought back.

How did he get out? she wondered. Is he all right? Is he warm? Has winter hurt him? Is he having the dinner of roast beef and gravy that he wanted so much? Is he among decent people who use courtesy and kindness?

What is kindness? Shall I ever know it again, now that Strat is gone?

The door opened.

For a terrible moment—the worst her soul had had —she wanted it to be Strat.

But it was a woman, thin and gray and angry, shrieking, "You cannot do this to me! I have done nothing to merit this! Let go of me!"

Of course Ralph and Dr. Wilmott paid no attention but enclosed her in the crib.

Katie turned her head. This is my life, she thought. One lunatic after another, their screams no different from the last set of screams.

Douglass made his lonely sounds and scruffled toward her and Katie tried to sing a song of comfort, but they were both beyond that now.

Moss fixed a pot of tea. She did not take a tray to Harriett and Strat. Annie was not fond of tea, which in her opinion was discolored water, but she enjoyed the heat of the pretty little cup and the act of holding its tiny curly handle as she lifted it in a ladylike way to her lips.

An hour went by.

Annie thought of Mexico, and warmth, and Harriett getting well.

"Moss," called Strat wearily from the sickroom. "Annie."

Harriett Ranleigh was dead.

She had managed to hang on for the only really important thing: the presence of the boy she loved. And when she had that, it was enough.

Death was not supposed to win!

Annie wanted to beat her fists against Death's chest, and kick Death in the shins, and shriek obscenities at Death. But Death had so obviously come for Harriett. There was something so completely missing from Harriett now. Not just breathing, not just heartbeats.

The beautiful soul of Harriett Ranleigh was gone forever.

Annie had never seen death. In her century, death was kept neatly in the hospital. You didn't actually ever get near it.

In 1898, death was casual. The nurse did not flinch.

177

Other patients, a man named Charlie and a girl named Beanie, were not surprised. Even Strat, who wept, was not shaken. The girl-like thing in his arms was no longer dear Harriett. He held her—it—for some time, and then gently lowered what had once been Harriett back into the pillows and kissed the forehead and did not let go of the limp hands.

Then he faced Annie. He did not wipe away his tears. They lay motionless on his face, defying gravity, a memorial to Harriett. "She gave you her love, Annie," said Strat. "She asked that I name my first daughter Harriett," he said, "and I gave her my word."

Annie could not look at them anymore. She stared out the window. White birches with black twigs gathered along a path. How feminine the birches were. Young girl trees. Harriett would not see spring. No color green. No sunlight on meadows, no birds singing, no warmth of summer.

If I had known, she thought, if Time had told me, I would have brought antibiotics and medications and cures. How cruel and vicious Time is, to let one generation get well, but not another.

Strat's eyes were shiny with grief. "Annie, without you, I would not have had this great gift. You gave me this. We made peace, Harriett and I, and I held her. She did not cross the bar alone. I was with her."

"You must let go now, sir," said Moss calmly. "I will prepare the body. Lockwood, I will need your assistance. Mr. Stratton, here is Miss Harriett's dear friend, Charlie, who will sit with you in your sorrow."

Florinda fanned herself. California was astonishing. Every single day it was warm. It never once rained and the sky didn't turn gray. Florinda felt that California had possibilities. Of course, they had no Society, and people here were vulgar. But each day you woke up with the sense that all would be well, whereas in New York you often woke up convinced that nothing could ever go well.

She could hardly wait for her stepdaughter, Devonny, to arrive. Florinda had met all sorts of adorable young men. They were all poor, and all needed Devonny's fortune, but that was to be expected. The important thing was, they were not Walker Walkley.

She pondered the mysterious telegram.

FLORINDA TELL DEVONNY HER MONEY WAS WELL SPENT STOP FIRST GOAL REACHED STOP MUCH LOVE ANNA SOPHIA.

Well, of course, Florinda remembered every single detail of the beautiful Miss Lockwood, and the scandal and the excitement and the chase! And most of all, the delicious hour in which *she*, Florinda, saved them all from evil.

Anna Sophia is back! thought Florinda. Her mind could not compass such an incredible thing.

Any message insisting that money had a good use and that people loved each other was a good message.

Still, Florinda wished she knew what the first goal was, and what the second would be.

"Florinda!" bellowed her husband.

She tucked the telegram safely away and hastened to his side. Hiram Stratton, Sr., had a very large side. He was consuming even more food and wine here in California than he had in New York. It was quite astonishing.

He just wanted to gaze upon her. Florinda did her very best to look lovely and pale. Staying pale was not an easy undertaking in southern California.

"I have just received a telegram!" he thundered.

Florinda quailed.

"My son has escaped from the asylum!" he shouted.

Florinda just managed not to smile in triumph. Undoubtedly, money well spent. "Ah, sir," she said to her husband, "it comes from your side of the family. That courage in adversity! That determination! That physical strength. That relentless quality."

He looked at her.

"No doubt," said Florinda serenely, "Strat has recovered. I am so proud of him. Are you not proud, Hiram? How lovely it will be to have your son back among us."

"He hurt Dr. Wilmott quite badly."

Florinda shook her head. "Doctor should have known better than to interfere with a Stratton." She kissed her husband's cheek. It was huge, and rolled down into more than one chin. She said, "We are blessed, aren't we, Hiram?"

Florinda felt the heat of the beautiful telegram in her pocket. She would spend the next few days saying fine,

fine things about her stepson, Strat. Then it would be time to begin saying bad, bad things about Walk. She beamed at Hiram. "How clever you were to come to California, my dear. The people here are quite dim. You have completely conquered them."

He glared, waving his telegram. "Did you have something to do with this?"

"Hiram, really. I'm only a woman. It takes a man to defeat walls and locks and chains and guards."

"This is true," said Hiram Stratton, recognizing the manhood in his son.

❧

"Hi, Mom," said Tod. "How's Tokyo?"

Apparently Tokyo was wonderful. Work was wonderful. Everything was very exciting. And how was Tod?

"I'm fine."

And was his father there in the house, as he was supposed to be? Mom didn't want to talk to Dad, or anything like that, she just wanted confirmation.

"Dad's here," said Tod cheerfully. "He's doing laundry right now."

"Your father is doing laundry? I find that hard to believe."

"Me too," said Tod. The person who found it hardest to believe was of course Dad himself.

"Let me talk to Annie," said Mom.

"She isn't around, Mom. I'll give her the message, though. She'll be sorry she didn't get your call." Big lie. The days were piling up and he didn't have the slightest idea where old Annie was. Tod hated her for it. But he wasn't going to have Mom out there on the other side of the world having kittens over it.

"Everything's cool, Mom." He told her about school, and his job at Burger King, and how the ice hockey team was doing.

"It doesn't sound as if you miss me at all," she said, too casually.

"I miss you a lot, Mom. Especially in the morning when I get up and it's cold and the house is empty."

"Empty?" she said. "But—"

"Of you, I mean. You know. No coffee perking and stuff." He was going to be almost as good at lying as his sister by the time his parents wrapped this up.

No.

Nobody could ever lie as much nor as well as Annie Lockwood.

Charlie listened to the description of the insane asylum. He was not sorry for young Stratton. Charlie didn't care how many excuses were produced; the fellow should have been at Harriett's side all along.

Charlie was full of grief.

He had seen so much death. And now Harriett was lost. Already the world seemed colder and thinner. Less worth the fight. One more good soul was gone.

Charlie was very, very tired.

For the first time, he admitted to himself that he was not going to make it either. He, too, would lie here forever, in the cold, cold ground, under the shadow of the mountains.

The Stratton boy stroked a brass ring four inches in diameter, thick as a thumb, hung with heavy, almost architectural keys. The doors they opened were probably just as thick and brutal as the keys.

Lockwood, the servant, came striding right up to them. When had this girl gotten off the boat? She was remarkably rude. Charlie could not imagine keeping a servant who spoke like that. "Listen, Strat," the girl said, "enough already. This is not my kind of thing, helping Moss with that. You get me out of this." Charlie could just barely follow her dialect. He had no idea what part of the country spoke like that.

Strat nodded and took her hand. "Come. The grounds are lovely. Let's wander. I have things to tell you."

Charlie was glad Harriett could not see how those two held hands. It was shocking, a man of Strat's station with a lower-class woman like that. On the other hand, she certainly was lovely, and Charlie had once had enough energy to be impressed by things like that.

Now he just missed Harriett. He wanted to howl like a wolf on the horizon, and let the entire heavens know that he opposed the death of Harriett.

Off the huge main building was a great covered porch, its screens stored for the winter. It would have a lovely view of the lake during the summer. Now it looked out only on snow, snow, and more snow.

Strat brushed snow from a bench, and they sat together in the heat of the sun, and were strangely warm in spite of the cold.

"Annie," he said.

It was bad news. She knew from his voice, quiet and determined, and from his face, held away from her. She had his profile, and not his eyes, and the profile was beautiful and the eyes full of secrets and pain.

She waited. His hands curled around hers as if he had never held hands before. "I love you. I love you completely," said Strat, and his eyes filled but did not overflow. "I love you forever."

There was a *but*. She already knew what it was. She had known since she stepped through Time. She shrank from it; she still thought there must be a way to defeat it. She wanted to be a daughter of the twentieth century and get what was hers. But she was here; a daughter of the nineteenth century; she must, instead, do what was right.

"But you must go home, Annie," he said. He had no air beneath his words, and the speech lay as faint as the cold mist before their faces.

"I love you too, Strat," she whispered. "Completely and forever." I want us to be *us*, she prayed. Please, please, let there be a way for us to be together.

He waited a beat before he went on, and it was the pause of gathering strength. It hurt him. "I must stay in my century, Annie. I have things I have to do."

"I could do them with you." Her voice was pleading, putting more burdens upon him, trying to force things to go her way.

"Yes. And that would be wonderful. Nobody would be better company than you." Strat was trying to smile, but it wasn't working; his face was falling apart in grief. "But you have your family to go to, and I have mine."

He was separating from her because of his family? These people who had hurt him so? "You're going to California?"

"No, no, not that family. I cannot make peace with a father who had me locked up rather than listen to my side of the story."

Annie cried, "But what about Devonny? What about your sister who *sent* me here? She loves you. She needs you, Strat."

Strat gave her the sweetest, saddest smile. "Devonny doesn't need me as much as she once did. You taught her something, Annie. You taught it to Florinda too. You taught them to be strong. They thought only men could be strong."

I was strong, thought Annie. Like my mother. In the end, the woman I admired most was the strongest. "And your mother?" she said softly.

"That hurts," he said. "But I cannot see her now. They would just find me. She will have to wait. The day will come."

It sounded like prophecy, like something already written, his mother waiting, and the day would come. Poor Strat's mother!

"I no longer believe that my father's money is worth having, and I will make no attempt to be his heir or his son," said Strat. "I know now what has worth."

"Love has worth," she said desperately, "and we love each other."

"Oh, yes," said Strat, and this time his full voice was there, declaring love. "Oh yes, we do love each other." He kissed her, and it was a wonderful kiss, but she was in too much anxiety to kiss back; it was his kiss, but not hers.

"I have debts, Annie," he whispered, "and I must pay them. My greatest debt is to you, for saving me. For bringing me to Harriett in time. I can never repay that. I can't even try. But there is one debt I can repay."

He was not going to tell her what the debt was. She knew from the farness in his eyes that the debt was his secret; and he would carry it through Time and history, and she would never know.

Please don't be a gentleman, Strat. Forget honor and valor and virtue. Forget debts. Stay with me!

But she said none of it aloud, for she would have to carry this secret through Time with her too: that she was not as nice as Strat; that she wanted herself and her plans to come first, not last.

"I want my previous life," said Strat, his voice breaking on the syllables, "to be history."

"History," repeated Annie. Why didn't people cooperate with her plans? Why must they always be themselves, instead of extensions of her?

"That's what I am to you, anyway, Annie. You told

me yourself. You looked me up in archives. Ancient dusty places where the records of dead people lie."

"You're not there," she said quietly. She had, after all, another parting gift for him. "You disappeared from the written record. I couldn't find you there. You are *not* in the archives, Strat. You are *not* in history."

"Really?" Strat was stunned and relieved. "No trial for attacking a doctor? No jail record?"

"Nothing they wrote about in the newspaper, anyway." He won't tell me his secrets, thought Annie, but I'll tell him mine. "My father damaged my mother so much, Strat. He damaged all of our lives. And I had to find out if I damaged the person I loved too. I had to find out if I'm just like my father—throwing away the things that count. I was so worried about you, Strat. I longed to see you, but I really came in order to see if it was my fault."

He had taken off the thick gloves. His cold hands cupped her cold cheeks. Two colds made a warm. She could have sat forever with those big strong hands heating her face. But they were done with forever.

"You didn't throw me away, Annie," he said. "You stepped back into your own Time. It took such courage. Last time, you were the one brave enough to know. You told me that you loved me enough to give me back to Harriett. Now I, too, am brave enough. We must part once more."

She would never hear a man speak like this again. A speech of poetry and honor. She took his hands and kissed his palms and the back of his hands and the flat of his thumbs and dried her tears against them. "What will you do?"

"I'm going to Egypt," he said, switching from poetry to adventure, and giving her the greatest grin on earth. "I'm going to excavate for mummies and kings. I'm going to find great tombs and the entrances to pyramids."

How could she agree never to see that grin again?

"I'll bet," said Strat, "if you look me up in books about Egypt, you will find me."

She swallowed. The swallow didn't happen. She was shut off from her heart and soul and hopes. She could only pat him and silently wish him well and weep for her own dreams.

"Do you still have money, Annie?" he asked anxiously.

She dug in her pocket. She had a hundred dollars. It was a fortune in this time.

"That'll be fine," said Strat. "I have money too. Harriett gave me all she possessed."

She did, too, thought Annie. Harriett died for him. She waited till he came, and she gave him her last breath, and her last love, and she took with her a promise: *name your daughter after me.* Whose daughter will that be? Not mine. He's sending me away.

"I wish I had something of you, Annie. I have memory and your stories. And I will hold you in my heart, but I would like a piece of you. But the clothing and the jewelry you are wearing are Devonny's, it is nothing of you."

She felt his waist. On the stolen brass key ring was a

pocket knife. For a moment she stared at the blade she switched out, the gleaming fearsome sharpness of it. Then she cut a lock of her long dark hair, wound it in circles, and put it in his hand. With both her hands, she closed his fingers over it.

When he opened his hand, the hair straightened itself, and hung, a black ribbon. "The color of mourning," he said. "I will mourn for you. For us."

There. He had said it. *Us.* The word she wanted more than anything else on earth. Two letters, she thought, and they matter so much.

"You will travel safely back, won't you?" he said, still anxious. "You did the other times. You'll just step through, won't you?"

She nodded. If Harriett, after all, could cross the bar to death for her journey, could not Annie cross the bar of Time for hers? How could Annie pretend to be afraid, when it was only Time she faced?

But she was afraid. If only she were with Devonny and Florinda, warm and sunny. If only . . . if only . . .

"I must go now," said Strat. "Walk and Doctor can't catch up to you, but they can certainly catch up to me. They will be here by nightfall, I am sure of it."

Once again, she had had only moments with him. Why did she always have to be strong? Why couldn't she be the one for whom it worked out, and was just right, and went on to happily ever after?

Being strong was tiring. You couldn't go on forever, being strong.

But I don't have to be strong forever, she thought

189

sadly. I just have to be strong till he's out of sight. Out of Time.

"You can step through easily?" he said once more. "You're sure?"

"I'm sure."

They stood together, in that awful moment of good-bye, when there is nothing left but one person leaving and the other person staying. "I love you," she said. The words seemed alive in the air, like the coming of snow. *I love you.*

"Safe journey," said Strat quietly. "I thank you for saving me and giving me that hour with Harriett."

She hugged him, and he hugged back, so tightly, and for a long time. There was a strange finality to that touch. As complete as doors shutting, or seasons ending.

It was forever.

"I love you, too, Annie," he said, "and I always will." It was the last thing he ever said to her, and then he drove away in the cutter, he and his dark horses vanishing into the trees.

☙

The father of Tod and Annie parked his car in the only shoveled parking area at the former Stratton estate.

The town had owned the place for many years. It had beaches, tennis courts and marinas, holly gardens and meadows for picnics.

In February it had the sad abandoned look of all New England halfway through winter. It looked, in fact, like his family. Strange and cold and separated.

There was something frightening about the picnic tables stacked behind the barns, tilted on their sides like huge wooden playing cards. The drinking fountains were wrapped in canvas. The snow-covered foundations of the old Stratton mansion were nothing but knobs under dirty snow. The little pond, where once Hiram Stratton had docked a yacht, was too salty to ice over, but it had the dingy crust of winter by the sea, rolled-up tissues of slush.

He was afraid to tell anybody that he was such a lousy parent, he didn't even know when his daughter had disappeared.

The fact that she had done this twice last year would work in his favor. They would say that Annie was bad: a runaway, incorrigible, worthless—a typical teenager.

He tried to decide what kind of parent he was. Bad? Incorrigible? Worthless? Typical?

He had come to Stratton Point as if he could find a clue in the spot where his daughter disappeared before. He found nothing but cold.

What'll I do? thought Mr. Lockwood. Call the police?

He wanted his wife. It had been a long time since he had felt that way.

Well, he was too little, too late. If he called her in Tokyo and said, Guess what? I have no idea where our daughter is and no idea when she left . . . No, this did not have the sound of apologies that put marriages back together.

"No, Mr. Walkley," said the village attorney calmly. "Miss Harriett Ranleigh did not leave her fortune to some ragged logger or some foul nurse. She willed her fortune to the Fresh Air Fund."

"What!" shouted Walk. "That liberal idiocy? City people who cannot be bothered to raise their own children properly? Immigrants and guttersnipes who expect their neighbors to do it for them? Disgusting little urchins with bad teeth and no morals?"

Both Dr. Wilmott and Walker Walkley were beside themselves. Money belonged to people who had money; it must never belong to people who did not. Walk smacked his palm with the side of his beaver hat. Doctor pounded his fist on the top of a high leather chair.

The attorney, some hack from the North, some small-town person who could not possibly know his job, failed to be impressed by the presence of Walk or Doctor. "I will ensure that Miss Ranleigh's wishes are carried out," said the attorney calmly. "Now if you will excuse me, gentlemen, I am busy."

They did not excuse him. They blocked the attorney's exit from Harriett's former sickroom. Already, the room had been scoured. Its next occupant would arrive on tomorrow's train.

"Who is this Moss woman?" shouted Walk. "I demand to see the viper who turned Harriett Ranleigh to this insanity."

Two servants cowered by the stove. Their exit, too, was blocked by Doctor and Walk. One was fat, the other thin. One was properly clad in starched white, the other by her bowed head and pitiful rags was probably a washerwoman.

"You may not lay a hand upon Moss," said the attorney.

But the fat servant turned out to be Moss herself. "Miss Harriett was proud to give her money to the Fresh Air Fund. She said that way she would have the laughter of children every summer."

Moss and the attorney looked at each other gladly, but Doctor and Walk looked at the woman in fury. Walk's skin grew red, his body literally flaming with lost hopes.

However, Doctor and Mr. Walkley were nothing now except blockades to getting the room ready. Moss was sick of them. "Lockwood," said Moss, "show Mr. Walkley to a guest room in the main building."

"Lockwood?" repeated Walker Walkley.

"Lockwood?" repeated Dr. Wilmott.

How they smiled.

CHAPTER 12

It was very late at night, almost dawn once again, but in the asylum, it was difficult to tell.

Katie did not look up when the door opened. Hope had dried like a leaf in autumn.

She could hardly remember autumn now. She had not seen one since she was little, and the stories she told Douglass about autumn sounded unlikely. Could trees really turn bright colors?

When hands circled her, Katie did not fight back nor question. She was accustomed to pain without explanation.

The hands stood her up, and a finger was laid on her lips, and now she looked.

She did not believe what she saw.

"It's me," whispered Strat. "Don't say a word."

In the cacophony of screaming, sobbing, chattering, mindless patients, this was a ridiculous instruction.

194

They both giggled. Their laughter blended into the laughter of hysterics.

"We're going to Egypt," whispered Strat.

This did not sound any more impossible than trees turning color. "All right," said Katie.

"You hold Douglass's hand. Otherwise he'll be difficult."

Katie held Douglass's hand. He was not difficult. He made his Strat noises and Katie promised to tell him a story soon. Although it was Strat's story that would be interesting.

Strat had simply unlocked the doors, knowing exactly where the attendants would be sleeping, for none stayed awake through the night. A patient who needed help in the middle of the night waited till morning. Or waited for days, depending on the mood of the helpers.

Strat quietly relocked each door behind them. Then they were outdoors.

Outdoors! Out of the asylum! Beyond the gates!

Katie felt winter wind, and bitter cold, and icy snow, and it was beautiful.

Two horses were tied behind black trees, and a sleigh with a cover, so she and Douglass would be toasty and warm and out of the wind. She stared. The black mane blowing in the wind. The scent of horse. The crescent of moon in the sky. The pattern of stars and the crackle of ice.

Strat boosted her into the carriage. "Clothing," he said, pointing to a small leather trunk. "I want you to look lovely."

I hardly even met the wind, she thought, as he shut

her out of the weather. What other adventures will I have? What else will I meet that I have never met before? "Strat, I may go to Egypt," said Katie, "but I will never be lovely."

"Harriett said your personality would make you lovely," said Strat. "She said to wear a heavy veil to keep away the gaze of strangers. You will be my sister, Katie, and Douglass, my brother."

Harriett's gowns for Katie, and Charlie's clothes for Strat and Douglass. He had packed swiftly, and with only Harriett for witness, and then Charlie. Not even Annie knew where he was now.

"But Strat," whispered Katie, "people will think ill of you, having a defective brother and sister."

"But I will be proud of myself," said Strat, "and Harriett will be proud of me, and we'll settle for that." And Annie? he thought. Annie, whom I could not tell? How will she feel, in her other century, with her other life? Will she honor me? Will she look in her archives? Will she remember my name and wonder about my fate?

"And a bath?" whispered Katie. "With hot water?"

"A bath," promised Strat. "With hot water."

"And roast beef?" said Katie. She did not actually remember roast beef, but Strat had talked about it a lot.

"Yes, and pie and ice cream."

Strat shut the door, and Katie held Douglass so he would not be afraid. The horses moved, and Katie and Douglass felt wonderful new things: rhythm and speed and bumps. They laughed, and together they touched every new surface and felt every new texture.

Never had Katie been wanted. Never had she hoped

to be all these at once: warm, clean, fed, clothed, and among friends.

"Thank you, Harriett," she whispered. "I will honor your name forever."

Outside, she thought she heard the howl of a wolf, and she was both thrilled and terrified.

But it was no wolf, raising its muzzle to the dark sky; it was Strat, like Charlie, without words for his grief. He had lost Harriett to death, and Annie to Time.

And he had loved her so, but it was his own words that had sent her away forever.

I had to save Katie, he told Annie, the tears he could not seem to prevent freezing to icicles on his cheeks in the mountain wind. You will be all right wherever you are, but she would not be.

And I owed her.

The world owed her, but it was my responsibility.

But Time did not come for Annie Lockwood.

She screamed and fought. She broke free of Doctor's iron grip. She kicked Walk brutally in the shins. She smashed the teacups and even grabbed the boiling pot from the stove to pour on them.

But she did not get free of them, and Time did not come.

The attorney and Moss and Mrs. Havers were very distressed. Charlie, outdoors on a chair, his man still putting glass bottles on the stone wall, listened to the commotion.

Strat, Strat, thought Charlie. You keep doing what

you think is best, but behind you, when you've shut the door, life chooses its own way. Its own terrible cruel way.

"You see," said Dr. Wilmott, "that she truly is insane."

"I do see," said Havers. "What a shame."

Annie faced the sky, screaming, "Time! Time! Let me through. Come for me!"

The sky, of course, remained sky. It did not speak, nor whirl forward in a tornado to whisk her away. They would have laughed at her had it not been so hideous. A lost mind was quite dreadful to witness.

Mrs. Havers said, "To think I would have hired her to work for me."

They all shook their heads sadly at the ways in which this girl had deceived them.

"Notify police at railroad stations," said Doctor, "that young Mr. Stratton will be attempting to travel. He is alone, out of money, and wearing clothing far too large for him." Doctor smiled at Miss Lockwood. "He won't get far," he assured her. Doctor said to Walker Walkley, "I shall capture young Stratton. It will be a great pleasure to me. I still nurse a wound and a headache. You must deliver Miss Lockwood to my institution."

How they smiled.

"Indeed," said Walker Walkley, "it will be even more of a pleasure to me."

Doctor sped away after Strat, whipping horses as cruelly as he had ever slapped a patient.

And Walker Walkley turned to Annie Lockwood.

They strapped her in a terrifying garment: a sort of bag, as if meant for a corpse. Her arms and legs were trapped within, and all the screaming in the world had no effect upon the harsh canvas.

Is this what Strat endured? she thought. But what Anti-Kidnapping League will come for me? I have no allies. My only ally is Strat, and he has left.

And Time, Time has left, too.

She tried praying to Time, like a god; and she tried threatening Time, like a bad boy; and she tried bribing Time, as if she had something Time needed.

Time ignored her.

Only the presence of Mrs. Havers and Moss and the attorney kept Walk from hurting her. But soon they would be out of sight of Clear Pond, and then Walker Walkley could do whatever he chose.

Each time she tried to change centuries, she merely convinced strangers that she was insane.

Moss, however, remained kind. She brought furs. "These were Miss Harriett's own," she said. "She would want to protect this sad creature from the cold. It is twenty below. Mr. Walkley, do take care of the poor thing. Do not let her escape. Death would be swift, in this cold."

"And we do not want death to come swiftly, do we?" whispered Walker into Annie's ear. "We want you to linger, don't we? We want you to suffer, don't we?"

Walk tied her canvas bag to the seat of the cutter and

carelessly threw a fur over her. "Think, Miss Lock-wood," he said, "of all the years you will spend in that asylum. And think, too, about Strat, whom you adore. He will join you soon. You will watch each other in Hell."

He set off.

How dare the bells still jingle and the horses still toss their beribboned manes? Annie was being turned into a lunatic, to be treated like an animal, and still there was music and beauty.

On Clear Pond, soft ice beckoned. If I could get Walk out on it! thought Annie. "Going over the pond would be a shortcut," she said, but she was too obvious, and Walk burst out laughing.

"Do you think I cannot tell that they have been cutting ice?" He shook his head at her dumbness.

The sleigh curved toward the steep hill that would take them away from cure cottages and toward Evergreen. The slope was covered with hay to slow the vehicle so it would not catch up to the horses and break their ankles from behind. Annie thought of what Walk and Doctor would do to her. Would they break her ankles from behind?

I am a twentieth-century toughie. I am not Harriett in a decline. I can escape.

Oh yeah? How?

She tried to think herself through Time, to hurl her body out of its bonds and across the decades, but nothing happened. She lurched against the bonds, but nothing happened. She screamed one more time, but nothing happened.

Walk flicked the reins and laughed.

She was his property.

She stared again at the wide, wide ice. Suppose she got free and ran across the pond. Would it hold her weight? Could she get to some sort of safety? And what if she fell through the ice? Would she freeze as she sank, becoming an ice coffin of herself? Or could she make herself fall through Time, instead?

Everything was so real. Too real.

The rough canvas.

The bitter wind.

She thought of the horrors in the lunatic asylum that Strat had described to her. *No. Not me.* She had not realized that she had mouthed the words until Walk laughed again, and shouted, "Yes! You!" He yanked the fur rug away from her, leaving her with nothing but canvas, at twenty below zero.

Then he half stood, adjusting Harriett's fur around himself instead of around Annie. It was a trophy. And she, she, too, was a trophy: proof that if he had lost fortunes, he had at least captured a victim.

∽✦∾

Charlie said to his man, "I really am an excellent shot." He took the rifle and turned slightly in his chair.

He said to dead Harriett, whose heart and goodness he still cherished, "I would have preferred to shoot Strat, my dear. But he did have an excuse. I had to accept his excuse, Harriett. Certainly you accepted his excuse. And I cannot let your Miss Lockwood suffer simply because Walker Walkley's greed was not satisfied."

Charlie pulled the trigger.

He really was an excellent shot.

He said to his man, "Go after the sleigh. Dump Mr. Walkley's body through the soft ice and free Miss Lockwood."

❧

Charlie's man said, "Sir?" He was very nervous. Very pale. Understandable. He had never before been employed by a murderer.

"Yes?" said Charlie. He desperately needed to lie down. His lungs would not accept this sort of activity. He was going to follow Harriett very soon. If only he could be assured that he would find her there, wherever death lay.

"Miss Lockwood is gone."

"What do you mean?" said Charlie.

"I don't know, sir," said his servant. "I released her from the restraints, and she gave me—sir, I did nothing to encourage it—she gave me a kiss and a hug. And then, sir, she was there . . . and then she wasn't."

Charlie was too tired to answer. Too tired to stay awake. So Harriett was right about that too. The Lockwood girl could travel through Time.

He wondered if death could be that easy. A shift through Time.

If so, Harriett, he said to her in his heart, I'm coming.

202

The fall was terrible, terrible.

The spinning was deeper and more horrific. There were faces in it with her: hideous, unknown, screaming faces of others being wrenched through Time.

I am not the only changer of centuries. And they are all as terrified and powerless as I.

Her mind was blown across like the rest of her. *Strat!* she screamed, but it was soundless. The race of Time did not allow speech. Her tears were raked from her face as if by the tines of forks.

It ended.

The falling had completed itself.

She was standing. Not even dizzy.

The fear of opening her eyes, and finding herself in the wrong place, or the wrong Time, kept her frozen, as if she had been thrown through ice, like Walk, instead of Time.

Strat, she thought, and the image of him was already distant: framed, like an old photograph on a grandmother's wall. Oh, Strat, you are the Past. Not the Present.

"Annie?" said a familiar voice.

She opened her eyes.

On the snow pack in front of Annie Lockwood was no cure cottage, no Clear Pond, no Walker Walkley, no horse and no sleigh.

Her own father stood before her, snow falling on his down jacket, the cute vibrant one he got to go skiing with his cute vibrant girlfriend.

Annie and her father stared at each other. She had no idea what story to make up, or what emotion to display. She had no idea what story she had just left, or what emotions she had been carrying.

It was just gone.

Strat and Devonny, Harriett and Moss—they were history now. And would she find Strat in archives? Would Egypt have his name?

He has my lock of hair, she thought, but I have nothing of him. Why didn't I take something of Strat? What will I have for the rest of my life?

Only memory.

"Annie?" whispered her father. He seemed afraid of her. His expression was exactly that of Charlie's manservant.

She was pretty sure that Dad was not going to want details on where she had been, or how she had gotten there and back.

Strat. In that syllable lay a hundred years of pain and loss. But love, too. She still loved him. Love had crossed Time with her.

But the part of Annie that had become a daughter of the nineteenth century vanished. In the twentieth century, you looked at things a little more harshly. Love is better, thought Annie, when there's a person to share it with.

A terrible, twentieth-century anger seized her: anger that she had not gotten her way.

From across Time came a vision of other people who had not gotten their way either: Harriett, Strat, Katie, Devonny, Florinda.

"We could have a snowball fight, Dad," said Annie at last. "Or fall backward and make snow angels. Which do you want?"

Her father swallowed. He swallowed a second time. He said, "It's probably my only chance to qualify for angel." He went first, trusting the snow to pillow him. In the thick white blanket, he waved his arms until the wings of angels appeared at his sides.

So Annie fell backward too. Their wings overlapped.

She thought of the lives she had invaded on the other side of Time. And for what?

So that others would have love.

For just the shortest moment in Time, but one she could hold, and remember, Annie knew that she really had been an angel: she had brought peace and safety and release.

She tried to reconcile her twentieth-century anger with her nineteenth-century courage. *I want love. I want love of my own! Here, in my Time. But it's Strat I want and he will be always, forever, in his Time.*

"I'm pretty confused, Dad," she said, after they had made a whole row of angels.

He said he was pretty confused too.

"But you're here, Daddy," she said, and suddenly she knew that that was a wonderful, wonderful thing: just to be here. She even loved him, which was a nice change from last year.

They got up from the snow.

How had Time done that: taken her from the Adirondacks to a New England beach to drop her down in front of her own father?

They linked arms and walked slowly back to the car, and she thought of the heater that would be in that car, and the cold, cold sleigh in which Strat had disappeared, and she put her arms around her father and sobbed.

"It's okay, honey," he said desperately. "Everything's going to be okay. Whatever went wrong, it'll be okay, I'm sure of it."

Annie was touched, that anybody could be sure that everything would be okay. Let it be okay with Strat, she prayed. Let it be okay for us too.

❧

"Show me the telegram," demanded Devonny. She could not get over the amount of sunshine they had here in California! It was delicious. You could almost taste it. It was unbearable to be swathed in New York layers when sand and palms and orange groves beckoned.

Florinda showed her the telegram.

"They made it," whispered Devonny. "Do you think we shall ever hear from them again?"

"Of course we shall. Your brother won't ignore his inheritance."

Devonny wondered.

"Anyway, there are other things to think of, Devonny." Florinda gave a little happy bounce. "I want to introduce you to a darling young man who was actually *born* here! In California!"

"One doesn't think of people as starting here," agreed Devonny.

"He's very civilized," said Florinda in a tone of surprise. "Eats with a fork and everything."

"Well!" said Devonny, laughing. "We'd better ask him over."

❦

"But what is that?" whispered Katie. She was getting used to the wonderful clothing now. The hat didn't fall off every time she moved, and the scarf didn't tug away, and she had finally trained Douglass to hang all over Strat instead of all over her. She was becoming quite judgmental of fashions. Hers were better than anybody's.

Katie loved the veil. Behind it, she could think clearly, with no interruptions from friend or foe who thought she was hideous. Inside the veil was safety.

"That," said Strat, "is our steamship."

Katie was awestruck by the size of it. A man-made transport that large? Surely Noah's Ark had not been so immense!

They had even seen Doctor at the train station. But he had not seen them, for Strat was a gentleman tilting a beaver hat to keep the sleet from his face, and Katie was a lady with a veil, and Douglass was a stumbling adolescent being a pain. Strat had bought a private room and from the safety of their very own room, they had watched Doctor pace the platform.

They left him there, looking for a lone young man in clothes that were too big.

How Douglass and Katie had loved the train! You

each had your own red velvet chair, and your view of an astounding world, and meals that came on trays. Hot, delicious, exciting, impossible meals. Wonderful new things like Coca-Cola and candy bars. And wonderfully, it was Strat who told the stories during their train ride. Stories to be locked up by, in Katie's opinion. Vehicles that flew in the sky, vehicles that needed no horses, vehicles that used no wheels, vehicles that did not even need roads!

Every night, instead of prayers, Katie thanked two girls she would never meet, for one was dead and one was Out of Time. Dear Harriett: I thank you for everything. Dear Annie: I thank you most of all, for courage, for Strat, for a chance.

"That ship will take us to Spain," said Strat.

"*Spain?*" It wasn't very close to Egypt. There were maps in Katie's Bible—she knew where these places were. There was the whole Mediterranean Ocean still to cross beyond Spain.

"That's all the ticket I could afford for three of us," said Strat, grinning and shrugging. "So in Spain we get off the boat—and, hey, who knows?" He was laughing now. "I'll have my sister and brother to support and I'll think of something." He stared at the Atlantic Ocean, and he was twenty-one years old and saw nothing but waves of adventure and challenge.

She looked at Strat, who had come back. Who had saved her. Who was kind, and believed in kindness.

And Katie knew that she was afraid of nothing.

Spain, Egypt, who cared? There was not a hole in the world that could compare to the hole over which she and Douglass and Strat had triumphed.

The ship's whistle blew long and strong.

Time to board.

Time, thought Katie, stunned by the beauty of good times. *My time.*

☙

Strat saw Katie and Douglass safely into their stateroom. Then he returned to the deck, and from a flower vendor rushing from dock to deck, he bought roses. Lovely soft pink roses. It was silly. He had no money to waste.

But it was not a waste.

The boat pulled away from America. From his history. From every footprint on the land where he and Annie had walked together. One by one, he threw the roses into the leaping winter waves. Good-bye, Annie, he said in his heart. Please love me anyway. I will always love you.

☙

It was summer before Annie Lockwood looked in the library again. The old room was hot and dusty, the scent of Time gone by.

The Egyptian collection was large. Everybody loves tombs and King Tut and mummies and the Nile. She checked every index of every book, and every reference in every article. No Hiram Stratton, Jr., ever appeared.

But Hiram Stratton, Sr., did. The century had changed, and in the year 1915, Hiram Stratton, Sr., died.

Annie finally stumbled on his obituary in the yellowing old newspaper pages: the long detailed column of his long cruel life. A successful life, for he had triumphed in money and land, invention and investment.

He was survived by his beloved daughter. There was no mention of a son.

So Strat had accomplished it, whatever that secret goal of his had been. He had stepped out of his own Time, as well as hers.

Annie Lockwood shut the last volume of newsprint, her final hope of seeing Strat's name in print once more.

Time kept all its secrets.

Except one.

The secret that she had loved him, each Time, enough to give him up.

Don't miss **Both Sides of Time,**
the exciting companion to *Out of Time*:

The room tilted and fell beneath Annie's feet.
Elegantly costumed people rotated like dressed mannequins, and the faces locked eyes on her.

What do they see? Do they see the witch that Bridget saw? Will they hang me? How do I explain traveling through Time?

"Get her!" shouted Mr. Rowwells.
They advanced like a lynch mob.
Her own long skirt was eager to trip her. It grabbed her ankles so they didn't have to.

I wasn't sent to make things right. I was sent to take the blame. I fell through Time in order to be punished for a murder I didn't commit.

❧

Caroline B. Cooney is presently working on
Prisoner of Time, the companion novel to
Both Sides of Time and *Out of Time*.

ABOUT THE AUTHOR

Caroline B. Cooney is the author of *The Voice on the Radio* and its best-selling companions, *The Face on the Milk Carton* (an IRA-CBC Children's Choice Book) and *Whatever Happened to Janie?* (an ALA Best Book for Young Adults). Her other young adult novels include *Driver's Ed* (an ALA Best Book for Young Adults, an ALA Quick Pick for Young Adults, and a *Booklist* Editors' Choice), *Among Friends, Camp Girl-Meets-Boy, Camp Reunion, Family Reunion, Don't Blame the Music* (an ALA Best Book for Young Adults), *Twenty Pageants Later,* and *Operation: Homefront.* Her time travel romance *Both Sides of Time* is the companion to *Out of Time.* Caroline B. Cooney lives in Westbrook, Connecticut.